STALKED

Alex Dean

TREBOR & TAYLOR PUBLISHING

First Paperback Edition: April 2015

Printed in the United States of America

Paperback ISBN 978-0-9905281-2-8

For my readers,
with my grateful thanks.

Prologue
Dr. Alexis Fields

MY EYES FLEW open to the sound of something or someone inside my condo as I lay asleep. Terrified, I began quietly easing upwards, my pulse hammering, back pressing against the headboard of the bed.

I immediately conjured thoughts of the torment and the harrowing past I so desperately wanted to leave behind. Something in my chest started to flutter. My eyes were wild as panic bloomed in the pit of my stomach.

Nervously peering across the room, I could now see a dark shape, smoothly and silently slinking about the doorway. Slowly. Moving closer—toward me. It was definitely moving, whatever it was, *whoever it was.*

Closer.

I lay there, paralyzed in terror as *it* crept closer. *Oh, God, no! This can't be happening!*

My heart raced as the masked intruder suddenly and swiftly lunged forward and violently grabbed me by my throat, pulling me out of bed as I tumbled onto the floor.

I screamed at the top of my lungs and tried to regain my balance as he held me down, one of his hands tightly gripping me like a horse's collar, the other pulling my hair back—commanding me to look up at him in horror.

My arms and legs flailing, I frantically stretched and grabbed the porcelain lamp from my nightstand, then managed with all of my adrenaline-fueled strength to swing, smashing it into his face.

The blow stunned him. He grunted and wavered momentarily. It was enough to allow me to free myself and run for the door of my condo to escape.

I unlocked the dead bolt and wrenched the handle, then darted into the hallway. I could hear him following close behind. I'd been able to move fast enough to get out before he leaped in a desperate attempt to stop me cold.

"HELP!! PLEASE!! SOMEBODY HELP ME!!" I screamed down the hallway, banging my fist on several doors as I ran toward the emergency exit stairwell.

I looked back and saw that he was still behind me. His face was hideously covered with some type of streaked silicone mask. He was dressed all in black. *Who the hell was this and why was he after me?*

I ran down the concrete stairs and hobbled out into the building's underground parking garage, panting, looking around for my car, for somebody, anybody to help me.

I bolted to Section C, the area where I last remembered parking.

I surveyed my surroundings, shaking, gripped in panic as I tried to get one of my car's doors open. *Dammit!* No keys. My eyes pinballed across the area. He was gone now. Vanished. Had he stopped chasing me? Could I have lost him somehow?

I felt a sense of relief as I crumpled down onto the cold concrete of the parking garage and nestled my back against the driver's side door of my BMW.

I closed my eyes for a split second to calm my frazzled nerves, wishing my pulse would simmer down. I took in a deep breath, silently wondering just what the hell was happening here. Was this all a bad dream?

Suddenly, I heard the patter of footsteps fast approaching, widely opening my eyes in fear.

I sat horrified and in shock as this monster stood before me with a sapphire-colored motorcycle helmet in his right hand.

Before a scream could escape my body, he abruptly lunged forward and furiously swung the helmet, aiming it directly at my skull—delivering a thundering *WHACK!*

My head snapped sideways, the bone-crushing blow rendering me senseless as I collapsed to the pavement.

I came to with blurred vision, a throbbing ache at the top left side of my head, and what looked like at least six human figures standing around me, staring as I lay semiconscious.

"Alexis? Alexis, can you hear me?" a woman in light blue scrubs inquired.

"Where… where am I?" I managed groggily.

"You were found unconscious in the parking lot of your building by a passerby. Somehow you suffered a serious injury to your forehead. A bleeding wound. Only God knows how you got there. Do you remember anything? Do you know what happened to you?"

"I… I vaguely remember running."

"What were you running from?"

"Running down the hall… from my condo," I murmured.

"Alexis, I'm Dr. Norvesh Patael," said a short, heavily accented man with a stethoscope, inching closer to the side of the bed. "We'd like to know who or what exactly were you running from?"

"Someone was chasing me. He… had a mask. I ran to the parking lot. That's… that's all I can remember," I slurred slowly.

"You're very fortunate your injuries were not more severe. You're suffering from cerebral edema. There is quite a bit of swelling in some of your brain tissue, along with some nasty-looking lacerations on the side of your head and the soles of your feet. I've scheduled an MRI for you first thing in the morning. We'll be monitoring you and running more tests to rule out any other complications. All things considered, I think your prognosis will be okay."

"Thank you, Doctor," I managed in a whisper.

"You're going to need some time off work, and the police will want to interview you to find out just what the hell happened."

A short and stocky nurse standing by quickly chimed in. "Alexis, I'm Frieda, the assistant on duty, and I'll be looking after you. Don't hesitate to alert me if you need help. We'll let you get some much-needed rest. Dr. Patael will be ordering more tests in the morning."

"Thank you," I replied as my eyes worked hard to stay open. Attentively, I watched each of them leave the room before nodding off into a deep slumber.

I tossed and turned, then awoke from what seemed like a terrifying nightmare around 3:30 a.m. My breathing was quick and labored. My skin was perspiring excessively.

I could still feel my attacker's hand around my neck. I'd envisioned him standing over me, this time naked, wearing that ghoulish Hollywood fright mask and holding what looked like a twelve-inch knife in his right hand.

Was it real? Had I been dreaming?

I could no longer sleep and quickly craned my neck toward the partially drape-covered window, yearning for a breath of fresh air.

I calmly lay there and took in a deep breath as I imagined the sights and sounds of Michigan Avenue. Shimmering street lights flickered in the darkness.

So much horrific violence and death struck the city every day, especially on the south and west sides, and now, here I lay, once again—a defenseless victim myself.

However, Chicago, with its gorgeous lakeshore, its vibrant nightlife and Magnificent Mile shopping, was still a beautiful place to be.

So… so beautiful, I thought… until Nurse Frieda was contacted by the Chicago police in an effort to interview me. They told her that Wilfred, my ex, might have been seen in the area.

How on earth could he have known I was here? And more importantly, *Does he know where I live*? He has promised to make my life a living hell.

I continued recoiling from the evil threat he had blurted the day he'd held that razor-edged knife to my throat. "*It ain't over*" still resonated in my head, leading me to believe it was true.

As my pulse raced.

CHAPTER **1**

Wednesday 8:40 A.M.

SARAH STALWORTH'S HANDS shook while she applied her mascara, eyeliner and lipstick as she readied for work as a communications specialist for a downtown transportation logistics firm.

She had managed to find stable employment in the River North area establishment, located in the trendy area just outside of Chicago's Loop. She would telecommute and did not have to appear at the office in person.

She worked alone from her near-North Side apartment, and only a low-resolution image of her face was visible over the company's network when she corresponded with other employees and clients of the firm.

This was almost perfect, she thought. She considered it one of the perks of the job. Priceless. Anonymity was key.

Today was going to be a new beginning, a renaissance of sorts in her sick and twisted mind. Work was not the real focus here. No, the real focus was murder. Simple, yet perfectly planned and executed, murder.

Some absolutely worthless, unsuspecting female victim, Stalworth thought. Not just anyone, mind you. One who would fit the necessary profile. One who would demand extraordinary attention from the media and police.

One who would make Sarah Stalworth Chicago's version of the Grim Sleeper Killer, only in a shorter amount of time.

She paced endlessly around her apartment before taking a seat in front of the widescreen all-in-one sitting atop the black corner desk in the living room. She calmly grabbed a nearby cup of cheap decaf, emptied two packs of sugar into it, and logged on to the internet.

Her background had been specific to computer programming, but she had accepted her current position with the understanding that she would be transitioned into a programming-oriented job once one became available.

She had not taken the time to do much in the way of socializing, but she expected that to change soon. The majority of her time had been spent surveying Chicago's dating scene, where she would engage her first victim.

Horny men who worked at the logistics firm found her attractive, in an odd and kinky kind of way.

They quickly became captivated with the new hire, seen only over their twenty-one-inch monitors. That seductive voice of hers, which sounded like one you'd hear on a phone sex line, was quite the turn-on, they thought.

They would send her suggestive personal messages frequently. But Sarah wasn't interested in them. She often spurned their awkward advances while keeping her preference for women a secret.

After she'd drained the disgusting cup of decaf, she logged in to an erotic chatroom she had visited often, eager to meet another woman for a one-night stand of carnal passion.

A small light hovered just above her avatar and indicated that she was online now.

"Hey, I like your profile and your picture, even though it's kind of blurry," said a young and attractive chatroom participant.

"Why, thank you! I like yours too!" Stalworth replied.

"Sooo many people don't post their real pictures. So, I just have to ask. Is that your real picture?"

"Of course. Don't be silly. That's why it's blurred. I can't risk being seen by people at my job. Even though they're all a bunch of perverts!"

"LOL. I know, right? You're funny."

"Freaks and perverts are everywhere. We have to choose our poison, I say."

"So what are you into? I can't tell much from your profile. There's not much to it. You like BDSM, or are you just into plain vanilla sex?"

"I'm open to trying anything. The naughtier and kinkier the better. It's all more satisfying that way. And I live for the thrill of it! What *is* life without adventure?"

"LOL! You certainly have an interesting way with words. I can't wait to meet you!"

"Ditto."

"Well, talking over the internet is safe, but *so* limiting. At least I think so, anyway. My friends all tell me that I need to stop being so rigid and live on the edge sometimes. That being said, I'm free tonight. Are you up to meeting at a public place to continue?"

"I sure am. And I was actually thinking the same thing. How about the Big Bowl on Ontario? I don't know how far you are from me now, but it's convenient, downtown."

"Okay. What time?"

"8:00 p.m. works for me."

"Sounds good, I'll meet you there at eight. I'll have on a faded denim outfit."

"Okay, cool."

Stalworth left her apartment, drove several miles over to Wells Street, parked in a nearby garage, and met young Taylor Hagenstock in the dimly lit restaurant in the heart of River North. The woman was cute in a schoolgirlish way, brunette, average height with a thin build.

The two hit it off and conversed at length, sipping pomegranate cocktails at the bar in between brief exchanges about each other's backgrounds.

Casual chitchat had become a precursor, a formality in such encounters before moving on to doing what they had both come to do.

A hostess promptly seated them in the dining room and they waited for a server to arrive.

"So, tell me a little about yourself. You ever been married?"

"No, as you can probably tell, I don't like men. And, well, I just haven't found the right person yet," Stalworth replied. "And you?"

"I was engaged to a wonderful woman once, but things didn't work out as planned. It was much easier for both of us to let go. Straight women that I know actually have a much harder go of it."

Stalworth's expression turned more serious. "It's such a bummer when that happens in life. I guess we just have to move on when it does," she replied.

"So true."

Hagenstock took a quick sip of her cocktail, lowering the glass as her eyes met Stalworth's. "So, tell me, now that we're here alone, what are some of your favorite fantasies? What kinky things do you like to do?"

"Well, I've always fantasized about meeting an attractive young lady, much like you, getting her alone and, well, doing naughty things to her."

Hagenstock smiled. "Okay, you've got me curious now. Like what? I want to hear it. What kind of things?"

"I'm embarrassed."

"Don't be. I don't kiss and tell."

"Actually, to be honest, I'd rather show than tell."

Hagenstock broke out into a hearty chuckle. "Okay, I like that. Well, we don't have to waste any more time here. Besides, I have a 10 a.m. start tomorrow. I'm filling in for my boss who's out on maternity leave," she said.

After the meeting, Stalworth walked the young woman out of the restaurant toward Wells Street, to the parking garage where she had parked her car.

While walking to Stalworth's vehicle, Hagenstock suddenly had an uneasy and eerie feeling come over her.

She had always met with other women at hotel rooms, but never had the courage to go to someone else's apartment.

As the two walked through the dimly lit parking garage, Hagenstock stumbled slightly, trying hard to maintain her balance. Her speech slurred. "I have to admit one thing. I shouldn't have downed all those deliciously tasty damn cocktails. That much I know for sure. I'll be paying for it with one bitch of a hangover in the morning. But at least it'll be worth my while tonight, right?"

"Yes. Absolutely. This will be a night you won't soon forget," Stalworth quipped, offering a smile. "Please, let me open that door for you, sweetheart."

Stalworth opened the door to her SUV for the woman, then patiently waited, holding it like a parking valet at a five-star restaurant.

As Hagenstock began to clumsily climb into the passenger seat, Stalworth pounced, blanketing her nose and mouth with a cotton pad doused with chloroform. Hagenstock, eyes filled with terror, arms flailing, breathing in the deadly chemical, quickly crumpled into Stalworth's arms. Stalworth managed to tug her limp body into the vehicle before peeling away.

CHAPTER 2

TAYLOR HAGENSTOCK'S PARENTS knew something was awry when their daughter failed to call or show up at work on Thursday morning.

In the city's cool predawn darkness, her nude and pallid corpse was found in a blue dumpster behind Empirical Furniture by several maintenance workers, who, after overcoming their initial shock, quickly called 911 to report the ghastly discovery.

Chicago police arrived within minutes and taped off the perimeter with yellow tape to prevent any passersby from contaminating the crime scene. Local reporters and news vans from CBS, NBC, ABC and WGN hurriedly descended on the block, as well as looky-loos from office buildings surrounding the area.

"Stay back," Chicago homicide detective Howard Beuregard barked at several bystanders as he exited his unmarked car and walked across the street to take in a closer view of the body. Beuregard was a seasoned veteran with numerous accolades to his credit during his twenty-three years of service and counting.

Pedestrians, blocked from walking near the crime scene, grew impatient, even belligerent. Beuregard turned from assessing the situation and abruptly stopped a young couple trying to meander their way through.

"Dude, my pregnant girlfriend's got a doctor's appointment across the street, and we need to get over there asap. It's urgent," said a spiked-hair rebellious type who looked like he could have fronted a wild heavy metal band.

"Well, your appointment is gonna wait!" the detective snapped back.

"Yeah? Well, thanks for the compassion, officer. I wonder if you'd say the same if she was one of *your* family members!"

"Look, asshole, we've got a murder here. *A murder.* I would say that takes priority over her doctor's appointment. And you want to talk shit to me about having compassion? Keep it up, and you and your girlfriend here will be wearing metal bracelets and spending the rest of the day in an eight-by-six lockup!"

"Whatever," the rocker mumbled beneath his breath.

Beuregard suddenly wheeled around and walked closer to the other cops and homicide detectives at the scene.

"Fellas, we got murders downtown now?" he called out to several patrolmen standing by.

"Well, we've got one."

Beuregard trudged closer and stood next to several crime scene techs, gazing in horror at Hagenstock's body lying amid piles of recyclable trash.

He shook his head. "Dammit! She looks so young and innocent. There are no defensive wounds or marks on her hands, feet or body. The ME's office should be arriving any minute. Keep the rest of those idiots across the street from coming over. We need to preserve this at all costs."

Hagenstock lay on her back, legs and arms splayed, her corpse semi-covered with scrap material, plastic and cardboard.

Her eyes were shiny and flat, frozen in time, still wide with fear from her untimely death that fateful night. Locks of her hair had been cut and her face had turned a horrid, bluish purple. There was a slight dribble of sticky fluid leaking from the right-hand corner of her mouth.

"Who found her?" Beuregard asked a uniformed cop on the scene.

"Some maintenance guys. They work at this place, Empirical Furniture. According to their witness statements, they were taking out the garbage after unpacking half a dozen sofas, and discovered the body when they opened the top of the dumpster."

"Anybody identify her?"

"Her wallet and driver's license were found on the ground in front of the container. Her murderer could have left them there or dropped them accidentally. Either way, Taylor Hagenstock's her name."

"I want as much surveillance video as we can get from businesses in the area. That's the first step, as usual. Has her family been notified?"

"Working on that now, Detective."

"Good. You guys are on the ball. The mayor's going to have major heat up our asses on this one. It's too close to home, if you know what I mean. I'm sure they're approving overtime as we speak."

"Gotcha. We're on it. Guys are canvassing the area now."

The buzz among the media hounds standing by echoed the inconvenient truth that it was highly unusual for such a crime to occur downtown, in the heart of the city, brazenly close to the rich and powerful and the most popular tourist attractions.

The mayor was in constant contact with Chicago's police superintendent, who put pressure on his top detectives to find answers. Quick.

Several miles away, Sarah Stalworth stayed holed up in her apartment, gripped by one of her maddening bouts of bipolar disorder, conveniently enjoying the luxury of not having to go out, as authorities sought to determine whether Hagenstock's murder was a targeted crime, or if she was the first victim of a deranged serial killer.

Her gaze was fixed on a nearby television, watching as special news reports interrupted regularly scheduled programming to discuss details of the grisly finding. "Lovely," she muttered as she zeroed in on every word that left the shaken, live-on-the-scene reporter's mouth.

She felt a rush of excitement. It was exhilarating and hilarious all at the same time. Moving to sit facing her computer, she turned toward the softly playing music in the distant background, the Gary Jules song, "Mad World."

She sang along hauntingly, "It's a very, very… mad world… mad world," as she adjusted her wig and removed the silk blouse from her large frame.

Suddenly, Stalworth stood from her office chair and strolled across the spacious room to look out of the apartment's living room window.

She peered in both directions, furtively surveying the tree-lined block. She was savvy enough to know that the police kept some information close to the vest. She would work hard to remain out of sight, for now.

She moved about this morning unflinching. Her pulse was still hammering. And she'd been smart enough *not* to bring Hagenstock back to her apartment.

"Nope, can't be that damn dumb! Not a chance!" she mumbled as she sat once again in her worn leather task chair, adjusting the height of her monitor, brightening the screen before she logged on to the internet.

There was more work to do, she thought. *A lot more to do.* This was only the beginning.

She ran the palm of her hand over the photos adorning the plaster wall alongside the computer. Each photograph was accompanied by a lock of hair from each victim. Her apartment had become a shrine to all the young women like the naive Taylor Hagenstock.

She despised them all, actually. Their pictures were neatly organized, from one side of the room to the other, all printed from their profile pages on the erotic chatroom web site which she had visited every night, looking for another helpless hack to murder.

She just had to know what they looked like. It was a simple rule. If there was no picture attached to a young woman's profile, the would-be sap did not exist, and the "unfit" prey would live to chat another day.

Stalworth *was* clever. Wickedly smart. She knew the type of mindfuck tricks that would make the most depraved of psychopaths blush with envy.

CHAPTER 3

Clear out…we're coming through!

CLEAR OUT! We're coming through!" the EMTs yelled as they exited the ambulance and zoomed through the hospital corridor to the ER, thrusting forward a gurney with a small body safely secured.

I watched in horror as I prepared to perform emergency surgery along with a team of experienced but frantic doctors and nurses.

My motivation for wanting to be an emergency room doctor was the same as it ever was. I wanted to help those who were sick, wounded, injured and suffering, on a daily basis.

But nothing in my medical training and my relatively short life span had prepared me for what I was seeing now.

A baby, clinging to life, had been rushed here after being shot in the head when her drug dealing father (and I use the term *father* lightly) held the child up as a shield during a shootout with police in the Englewood neighborhood.

The asshole almost got away, hurling the child to the ground like a piece of garbage before turning to run through a gangway.

We owed this little angel every opportunity there was, and we gave her our best efforts. Truly we did. But this precious gift to us didn't make it. She never had a chance.

When she was officially declared dead, I felt as if someone had literally gutted my insides. I shook and quivered. Sometimes I wondered if even I would make it through witnessing this horrible situation.

A vivid snapshot of her lifeless body remains ingrained in my psyche. She lay still and peaceful on the blood-soaked gurney, her eyes closed, another senseless victim of these mean city streets.

The girl's family had been given the terrible news but had somehow been blocked from entering the emergency room. They shuffled throughout the corridor outside of the ER, screaming, sobbing, visibly upset.

And understandably so. A young woman wearing a pink jogging suit and denim jacket had to be held back by two of the hospital's security officers. She had identified herself as the child's mother.

"Let me see my baby! I wanna see my damn baby!" she shouted, trying her best to break free of the officers' grips—to bolt forward twenty paces to the emergency room.

I walked over to the young woman. I'd heard someone refer to her as Chantel. She was inconsolable.

An older man with white hair, wearing a black leather coat, an argyle sweater and dress slacks—probably an uncle or the grandfather—and another woman bookended her, trying their best to keep her from crumbling to the floor.

"I'm Dr. Alexis Fields. I'm so sorry for your loss," I said gently.

She glanced at me, wiping tears away as they fell from her cheeks. "Thank you. That little girl was all I had, my heart... soul and joy. And now she's gone. This ain't right," she said, shaking her head solemnly.

I put my hand on her shoulder as my falling tears matched hers. "Please know, we did everything we could. This hurts me more than you could imagine," I offered.

"All he had to do was keep my baby out of it!" Chantel cried out.

"Who? Who are you referring to?" I asked.

"Anthony... Anthony Burton. He's Alisha's father, even though he never did anything for her. He got outta prison, out on parole. We hadn't talked much since he started his sentence. But he contacted me last week and I agreed to let him see her. What a dumb mistake that was. He's still the same loser he ever was. Ain't changed a bit. He gave me some line about how he changed while he was in prison, turned over a new leaf. And now this."

"Were the police able to catch him?" I asked.

"Yeah. They got his ass. Just what he deserved, too. What so-called father holds his kid up as a shield while he's being shot at by the police? Tell me, do you know?"

I wished I had answers. Something I could say that would offer some sort of comfort during this difficult moment. But there were no words that I or anyone else could say to make what had happened seem any better.

"My prayers are with you and your family. Please let me know if there is anything that I or my staff can do to help."

Chantel nodded in agreement.

Other family members were consoling each other, hugging whomever they could as several nurses looked on, wiping streaming tears from their own faces.

An elderly woman, possibly the child's grandmother, had to be held up. "Oh, Lord," she groaned when she heard the news. I hurried over to her and draped my arm around her shoulders.

"I'm so sorry. We did everything we could to save her," I said.

She looked at me and nodded. The expression on her face was one I'll never forget. The pain and grief she felt were evident.

I left the ER an emotional wreck. This was part of the job I'd expected. What I'd signed up for. But seeing death up close and personal took some getting used to, especially when it involved a child.

After gathering myself, I was making my way down the hall for a meeting with staff members when I got a phone call from a journalist. She worked for a women's magazine and wanted to do a cover story about women who were able to overcome the emotional trauma of being sexually assaulted.

They had heard about my story—and the fact that I had become a doctor made me an impressive subject, she told me. Perfect for sensationalizing my plight, and to sell more magazines, no doubt.

I figured it would be a good gesture on my part, especially if my experience could be of help to countless other women who had been raped.

I felt comfortable and elated, and agreed to meet her at my condo on Monday at six in the evening to do the interview. She mentioned that a photographer would accompany her to take some pictures.

This was a big deal, and I told most of my colleagues as I encountered them throughout the day. I couldn't resist seeing them wince with envy.

Jasten Wier, a young nurse practitioner who'd been recently hired, walked toward me as he passed a bank of elevators. He'd always glance at me from head to toe and never missed an opportunity to throw a flirtatious comment my way.

"Alexis, you've got to be the most gorgeous doctor in all of Chicago. So when do I get put on the list of guys waiting to take you out?" he joked.

"I'm afraid you'll be waiting indefinitely, Jasten. The list is that long," I answered with a chuckle. "Besides, I've got expensive tastes. Think you can afford me?"

"For you I'd give it a try. And only for you!" he responded with a smile before turning toward the hospital's Center for Coronary Disease.

CHAPTER **4**

AFTER BEING DISCHARGED from the hospital, recuperating for close to a month, and then returning back to work, it was a relief to be at home these days, especially when you considered it was completely voluntary. I had been sitting pensively in my living room for the past two hours, watching live protests on CNN regarding police-involved killings while waiting for the journalist from the magazine's editorial department to arrive to do the feature story on my ordeal in Lake Park.

I turned off the television, quickly reminded of my own less-than-ideal encounter with that monster of a cop, Mike Crowley, and the Lake Park police.

I was definitely in a better place now.

And it was time I put a positive spin on a negative experience, I thought. But it was now twenty-eight minutes after six and I hadn't heard from anyone.

No phone call to say they were late or couldn't make it? How strange. I had given them the correct address, hadn't I?

I peered out of my door's peephole and didn't see anyone, but I could hear footsteps trudging down the hall. The footsteps came closer. Could that be the journalist and her photographer?

I opened the door with anticipation. Suddenly, I stammered in fear. There was a strange man standing in the hallway. He abruptly stopped, glaring at me with a look of astonishment.

This guy looked to be about fifty-something, about six feet tall, with piercing dark eyes, clean-shaven, wearing a navy blue Adidas jogging suit and a pair of scruffy white Reebok cross-trainers. There was nothing in his hands except for a sheet of paper.

"Alexis Fields?"

"Yes, and you are?"

"The name's George. Shit, you're much better looking than I anticipated. I'm here about your personal ad on Craigslist."

"What ad? What are you talking about?"

His eyes narrowed. "The one about your secrct, dark, twisted fantasy," he said, and smiled wickedly.

"Excuse me?"

"Look, I know you might be a little timid or maybe apprehensive, even. There's no need to be, sweetheart. I'm not some sadistic maniac or killer."

He continued, "See, I'm only looking for some risqué fun, and, well, I saw your ad about your willingness to role play, where you're the victim of a sexual assault and I'm the would-be attacker. It's right here. This is the ad," he blurted as he held out the piece of paper for me to examine with my own eyes.

I slowly extended my hand to grab the paper from him so I could see for myself while keeping my gaze fixed on whoever this creep was.

I shuddered as I read in total disbelief…

HORNY GAL READY TO PLAY! RECENTLY RELOCATED FROM WISCONSIN. IN NEED OF BEING SEXUALLY ASSAULTED TO FULFILL A DARK, TWISTED FANTASY. ONLY SERIOUS AND WILLING PARTICIPANTS NEED RESPOND. CONDO BLDG NEXT TO WHOLE FOODS. COME BY AFTER 6 PM AND GO TO UNIT 506.

My eyes welled with tears. My heart raced. I was overcome with emotion as I struggled to tell this guy to get the hell away from me.

"There's been a mistake. I did not put this on Craigslist!" I yelled at him before sprinting back into my condo. Someone else had obviously done it as a prank, and I had a damn good idea who it was.

I did what I usually did when I was upset, and that was either to call my mother or my friend Carol, who was always there for me, even through the most troubling of times.

I couldn't reach either and decided to go for a walk. I needed some fresh air. I needed something to eat, even though I didn't have much of an appetite.

After grabbing my car keys, I bolted out of my unit and headed down the hallway toward the elevators to reach the underground parking lot.

It was a briskly cool night, eerily dark. Several street lights on the block had blown, and the terrifying thought of Taylor Hagenstock's body being found in a dumpster not far from here came to mind, as well as my own fear of Wilfred.

He *must* know where I lived. I was sure that in his sick and twisted game of vengeance, he had fiendishly set up the fake ad on Craigslist.

My intuition told me to call and check in with Lou Haney, the detective I had met when Bill Finnegan was brutally murdered across the street from my childhood home in Madison. If anyone knew the latest about Wilfred, it would be him.

That would have to come later. For now, someone else was in this parking garage. I glanced at a man staring at me from a distance, watching as I climbed into my BMW. Then he disappeared. Maybe another freak from the bogus Craigslist ad.

Fortunately I wasn't alone anymore. I turned around and saw a young black kid I knew who lived in the building.

Terrell Burton was his name. His mother was a lawyer and his father a Cook County judge with quite a reputation among the women who worked in Chicago's judicial system.

Terrell's father, the Honorable Tobias Z. Burton, had been caught having a threesome with two of his clerks in his chambers during a court recess last year, but in consideration of his long and illustrious career on the bench, he was only reprimanded.

"Hi, Ms. Alex," Terrell said as he approached. "Ms. Alex" was a nickname he'd given me. He'd said it was cool. I could go with that.

"Hi, Terrell. What's the latest?"

"Good things, Ms. Alex. I made my high school's football team, first string! That means I'll play in most of the games unless I get hurt," he said, beaming with excitement.

"Well, good for you, Terrell. That's quite an accomplishment! Now, if you do get hurt, you know I've got your back."

"That's good to know, then," he responded with a chuckle.

"So, what position do you play? Quarterback? Running back?"

"Nah, safety. Coach said I was better on defense. My mom drops me off at practice, and she agreed that I looked pretty good in the secondary too."

"That's good to hear. Your parents must be very proud of you. Let me know when your team is scheduled to play. I just may come to one of your games on my off day."

"Hey, are you expecting someone?" Terrell asked, looking over my shoulder.

"No. Why?" I replied, my smile turning to a look of concern.

"There was a guy standing by the elevators and he asked if I knew the woman who lives in 506. I told him I didn't. Hope I did the right thing."

I smiled. "You did, Terrell. Thank you for that. There are some bad people out there. Some who would like to harm me. So let's look out for each other. You watch my back and I watch yours. Is that a fair deal?" I said, extending my fist for a bump.

"Yep, deal."

CHAPTER 5

FOR SOME ODD reason, Taylor Hagenstock's murder stayed with me. As I drove by Wells Street where her body had been found, I could feel a connection. I could feel her presence in some weird way.

It was a voice crying out in desperation, pleading for justice: *I didn't deserve this.* She reminded me a lot of myself: a young, upwardly mobile brunette, with an eerie resemblance I'd seen when her picture was scattered across the media.

Her murder, on top of the fear I'd already had about Wilfred and what he might do, constantly kept me living in a nightmarish hell.

I didn't even have the desire to date anyone right now. "People are fucking crazy these days!" I ranted to myself.

When I had first met Wilfred, he'd had his quirks, but I'd never imagined the horror of what he could or would turn into.

Signs. There are always signs. And I had magnificently failed to see them.

My family and friends had warned me to stay away, especially after seeing him at his timorous best. He'd been clearly pegged as a mama's boy. He could never, not ever, make one damn decision without consulting her first!

It was her he consulted when he wanted to know where to take me for the weekend of my birthday. It was her he consulted when he thought about where we would go for our honeymoon once we were married. And it was her he consulted when he contemplated whether he wanted to have children or not. *Are you friggin' kidding me?* I thought. What thirty-five-year-old man did these things?

And there was another side to him that should have been cause for concern. He could be so damn selfish and petty, especially when it came to money.

If I hadn't known any better, I would have thought I was dealing with someone half his age. And I'd have sex with him whenever he wanted.

Maybe *that* was the problem. I'd fucking spoiled him. He was already used to getting his way. When he lost his job, I was there for him and even helped him to look for another.

I'd nurtured him. Yeah, maybe that was part of it too. Men these days had been conditioned to think they should be catered to. And why not? There were plenty of willing women waiting in line—up to the task.

Bored, I strolled over to the Macbook Air perched on the glass and metal cocktail table in my living room. After reading about the latest celebrity breakups and divorce rumors in Tinseltown, I went into my inbox to read the new email I'd received, and found something from my friend Carol with an urgent message in the subject line: YOU NEED TO CHECK OUT YOUR FACEBOOK PAGE! HURRY! She'd sent the note from her iPhone, and said she couldn't call because she was heading into a meeting at work.

What the hell could be so pressing that Carol would send this with such urgency? I quickly logged on to Facebook, to get a look at whatever Carol had seen— and I was flabbergasted. My face flushed with agitation.

Recently posted at the top of my page's Timeline was an uncompromising close-up—of my mother, buck naked from head to toe, taking a shower, with the outrageous caption: A COUGAR IN THE HEAT OF SUMMER.

I had a lump in my throat. My hands trembled. I frantically managed to get through the steps to delete the humiliating picture, but the post had already been shared with plenty of people I knew.

I was grotesquely embarrassed, and quickly sent out a message to all of my "friends," informing them that my account had been hacked, and to please delete the photo from their profiles and hard drives. I could only hope and pray I'd have any luck with that.

My stomach churned in disgust and my heart felt like it had crumbled into a million pieces. I was burning mad and decided I'd had enough, all while looking for Wilfred's phone number.

I wanted to curse him out so badly, to rip his fucking heart out, if he even had one, but decided to keep my composure and not give him anything to use against me.

Somehow he'd gotten a chance to take the scandalous picture when he was at our house. He must have been saving it for exactly "the right occasion." What a tool he'd turned out to be!

CHAPTER 6

SAMANTHA COLLIER WALKED hurriedly to her black 2012 Toyota Camry after leaving a parent-teacher conference at her son's school on the South Side. The boy's lack of attention and inability to focus in class had warranted the impromptu meeting.

Collier herself was an intelligent and attractive woman, slender and sleek, with porcelain skin and raven black hair.

She was wearing a two-piece black pant suit with a heather gray wool overcoat and walked fashionably in a pair of Christian Louboutin pumps.

She fidgeted with her keys as she walked out of the building and into the cool of the night, plodding closer to her vehicle, which was parked in the visitors' lot outside of Oglesby Elementary.

Watching her intently was Sarah Stalworth, who was sitting in a car several parking spaces over. She had taken her time, done meticulous research, and gotten to know a lot about Collier.

She knew that Sam (as her friends liked to call her) was a divorced single mom and lived with her son in the Prairie Shores apartment community.

Stalworth had dreamed of this moment for the last two weeks. Gosh, it was such a rush. The thrill of the hunt. She lived for it. Another chance for a rise in the limelight. And this would be so damn extra special! Stalworth had picked Collier out specifically.

She had decided to murder the young woman who had worked for the Mayor's Office of Special Events for the past fifteen years. Collier was a dear and close friend of the mayor himself.

Imagine that. A victim right under the mayor's nose. *What could be better than that?* she thought.

This was exciting, like a scene out of those Liam Neeson movies she was so enamored with. Was it *Taken?* Or *Taken 2?* Didn't matter!

As Collier cautiously inched her car forward to turn and exit, Stalworth pulled out close behind her, following the unsuspecting city worker onto Green Street.

She tailed Collier as she meandered through traffic, finally arriving at her apartment building at ten minutes to six.

She watched as Collier began to exit her Camry to walk into the foyer of her building. Several seconds later, Stalworth stiffly climbed out of her vehicle and walked into the building, confronting Collier before she entered the hallway.

"Ms. Collier?" Stalworth asked after following her inside, her face pretending at sincerity.

"Yes. Can I help you?"

"I wanted you to have—"

"Yes? What is it? What do you have for me?"

Collier gasped, looking mortified as she glared at the madwoman suddenly coming her way.

Stalworth moved quickly to the side and then forward. With one swift kick, she sent Collier stumbling backwards, crashing hard to the tile floor.

Then she pulled out a Tac Force folding knife from her purse and furiously plunged the steel blade into Collier's chest. She thrust the weapon upwards, vigorously to the left, then down diagonally to the right in a frenetic sweeping motion.

Collier's eyes flickered. Several small, guttural groans escaped her airway as she clutched the blood-soaked point of entry. She managed a desperate, life-sucking gasp as she let out her last breath.

Stalworth had done it again.

Another one down.

CHAPTER 7

POLICE HAD BEEN called to the scene of the Collier murder within minutes of the body being discovered by a terrified resident of the apartment building.

A crowd had gathered. There was a diverse group of onlookers comprised of all ages, some white, mostly black.

The looks of concern on their faces were evident. This was something that mostly happened in other parts of the city, in less-traveled neighborhoods.

Detective Howard Beuregard received the call, quickly got into his unmarked police unit and drove the several miles to the South Side.

He had been assigned to lead the team of specially-appointed homicide detectives chosen to work the case.

Other responding officers pulled up in front of the apartment complex in patrol squads and unmarked vehicles. With guns drawn, they quickly filed inside the building's lobby. Collier's body lay perched up against the glass entrance door of the hallway. Visible entry wounds were apparent in her stomach and upper torso.

The light gray marble floor that adorned the building's entrance had been completely slathered with blood.

EMTs arrived at roughly the same time as the police and quickly signaled the grim indication that Collier had died from her stab wounds.

The officers stood pensively inside and outside of the entrance, taking turns closely viewing the body as crime scene techs took pictures, dusted for prints, and painstakingly looked for any other crucial evidence that could be retrieved.

"Shell casings?"

"None."

Beuregard hunched down and got within a foot of the crumpled corpse, peering at Collier's torso in the dimly lit vestibule with his Maglite.

"She's been gutted," he said, as he looked closer at the manner in which the wounds had been administered.

"Sheesh, the way these wounds look says one thing, that her killer committed this act in a fit of rage."

"Yeah, I'd sure as hell say so."

Beuregard looked around the entrance and noticed something that caught his eye.

"There's a tiny camera up in the corner. You see that?"

"I do. Let's hope it's working."

"If so, we need the footage asap. Who here has the contact information for management?" Beuregard asked as he walked back outside.

A frightened woman calmly took several steps forward, nervously identifying herself as Charmaine Wilds. "I can help you, sir. I work in the management office. Residents notified me when the body was first discovered."

"I'm Detective Beuregard, Ms. Wilds. Any idea if that camera is working?" he said as he pointed toward the ceiling in the vestibule.

"I believe so. I can call the security company that handles our surveillance equipment and let them know you need it."

"Good. We'll also need access to the victim's apartment."

Wilds' eyes widened with fear. "I don't know," she said nervously.

"You don't know? What do you mean, you don't know? It's imperative to our investigation that we get inside her apartment."

"There were rumors about Ms. Collier's lifestyle."

"What do you mean? Talk to me. What rumors?"

"Residents in the building had often seen her with what looked like unsavory characters. The kind of people folks like me don't want to mess with. That's the reason for my reluctance in getting involved, Detective."

"You're scared. Okay, we can handle this another way. Either way, we're getting in there. Now I need for you to unlock the door."

Wilds shook her head in a display of defiance. "I seriously don't want to get involved."

"I'm not asking you, Ms. Wilds. I'm telling you to provide us access to that apartment, now!"

Wilds reached in her right-hand pocket and pulled out a set of keys, and started inside to open the door to Collier's apartment.

Beuregard took in a deep breath, ready to explore any new direction the case would lead.

The clock was ticking.

CHAPTER 8

"ALEXIS FIELDS, YOU'RE under arrest…"

I'll never forget those words I heard so effortlessly blurted from the cop's mouth shortly after I'd arrived at work.

"Are you kidding me? I'm *under arrest?* Oh, hell, no! You guys have got it all wrong. You see, Wilfred, my ex, is the one who should be under fucking arrest," I yelled to the police who had bulldozed into the emergency room to arrest me. "What am I being arrested for?"

"Suspicion of murder," one of them barked, grabbing for my arm.

My heart sank. It felt like it was going to explode in my chest.

I hyperventilated, trying to control my emotions to respond sensibly as one of them unhooked his cuffs from his belt and asked me to turn around. "You guys are making a big mistake! I can explain all of this."

"You might want to make other arrangements with the hospital, Doctor. You're going to be gone for awhile," one smart-ass cop quipped.

I wanted to kick him in the balls and see him wince with the same pain and embarrassment that he'd inflicted on me. And why did it take six cops to come and arrest me? *Am I that much of a badass?* I thought.

"Let's make this easy on her, guys, at least until we get her out of the hospital," one of them muttered. Could this asshole be any more cynical?

I was escorted out of the ER, out of the hospital and into a waiting squad car. I was completely embarrassed as my staff of nurses and other hospital personnel stopped what they were doing and looked on in bewilderment, wondering what I'd been accused of—or worse yet, what I had done.

We slowly left the premises and meandered through a wave of pedestrians in what was now rush hour traffic, over to 1st District Police Headquarters.

This is all some type of misunderstanding, I kept telling myself. I was eager to know why I had been arrested and needed to be questioned.

Two officers gently escorted me out of the back of the squad car, into the station, and down a utilitarian-looking corridor, straight to an interrogation room, where one of them politely asked me if I needed anything.

"Only to know why I'm here," I scolded.

"You familiar with the Hagenstock case? Girl who was murdered downtown?" a tall cop with hazel eyes and a buzz cut asked me.

"Yeah, it's been all over the news," I said. "I was sorry to hear about it. But what's that got to do with me?"

"Well, a lot, actually. Our forensics team went through the profiles of a website that Ms. Hagenstock was a member of. She was communicating with another member of the site, and the two of them arranged to meet in person at the Big Bowl restaurant. That name ring a bell?"

"I've heard of it, yes, but I've never been there."

"As it turns out, Dr. Fields, the person Ms. Hagenstock hooked up with goes by the name of Sarah Stalworth, with a physical address and computer footprint matching yours."

"Okay, I get it now. You guys don't understand. I have an ex-boyfriend who's out to destroy me! He's been hacking into my accounts, posting fake ads on Craigslist using my address, and even put a picture of my mother naked on Facebook!"

The cops broke out in hysterical laughter.

"This is not a game here! My life is being destroyed by this loser and you guys think it's funny? If you'd bother looking into this in more detail, I'm sure you'll see that I'm innocent and clearly being framed."

"Would he go that far? To murder someone and make it look like you're the perp? How do you know your ex-boyfriend is behind any of this? Tell us, how?"

"I recently moved here from Lake Park. I'm originally from Madison, Wisconsin. Before I left Wisconsin, I ended the relationship with him."

More cops crowded into the room, listening intently, still with smirks on their faces.

"Being the sick son of a bitch that he is, he didn't take it very well, and he attacked me. Put a knife to my throat. I filed a restraining order. He threatened that this whole thing wasn't over, and that he would turn my life into a living hell."

"Anything else?"

"I might also add that a neighbor across the street from where I lived, Bill Finnegan, came to my defense during the attack and he ended up being found brutally murdered on his front porch."

"Okay, we get that. But what alibi do you have that exonerates you and puts your ex behind any of this, including Hagenstock's murder?"

"Because I didn't do it! I've never met or seen that woman in my life! You have to believe me!"

"We can understand your ex, in his horrific way of thinking, would want to exact revenge against you. But why would he go after Hagenstock? It doesn't make sense."

"I have no idea. Apparently, that's something you guys need to figure out," I scoffed.

"Well, it is. But part of the process of figuring things out involves interviewing potential suspects, persons of interest, which brings us to our little meeting here today. How do you even know he's in Chicago? You said he lives in Madison, Wisconsin. Is that correct?"

"Well, he did. But when I lived in Lake Park, I received a phone call from Lou Haney, a detective in Madison who was assigned to Bill Finnegan's murder. He warned me to watch my back. The police in Madison had no clue about Wilfred's whereabouts, then, or now."

One of the detectives in the room took notes, following my every word.

"You guys should know, I was recently assaulted in my condo by an intruder. While I was lying in the hospital being treated for my injuries, Frieda, a nursing assistant, was contacted by someone, allegedly from the Chicago police, informing her that Wilfred had been seen in the area. The message was eventually relayed to me. So it stands to reason that he could know where I've relocated to, and followed me here to Chicago."

"What's his full name again?"

"Wilfred Bachman."

"I'm sure you realize the importance that's been given to solving this case, Dr. Fields. We're awaiting further forensic results from DNA samples obtained from the body."

"I would like to add, from the pictures I've seen of her on television, I thought she closely resembled me. Not that it matters."

"Well, it could matter. Whoever the perp is, he could be going after women who fit a certain profile. That's not uncommon."

"I never saw Wilfred as a murderer, which makes this whole thing so strange," I said.

"A lot of perps guilty of murder start off on a smaller scale. They become increasingly depraved in their sick and twisted minds, eventually escalating to more heinous crimes," one of the detectives replied.

"I didn't do this! You have to believe me!"

"It'll be a few more days before we gather additional information and possibly clear you. In the meantime, if you have an attorney, Dr. Fields, you're free to make a phone call."

I sat there in the interrogation room wondering how everything had come to this. My mind drew a blank as I looked at these officers who had accused me of this most unthinkable crime.

The first person I wanted to call was my mother. After leaving home and starting this arduous journey on my own, my life had been anything other than ideal up to this point.

It was imperative that I cleared my name. Fight back. *No, Wilfred, you're absolutely right. It's not over!*

CHAPTER **9**

HOMICIDE DETECTIVE Howard Beuregard came to work to find the normal stack of mail waiting on his desk. After grabbing a cup of coffee, he sat down and sifted through the typical pile of police, legal and administrative correspondence.

Everything looked like the usual fare, except for one particular envelope that stood out with some unusual typed text in the "addressed to" field. The envelope did not have a return address.

He picked it up and closely examined it, bewildered. It had been oddly addressed to the Chicago Police with his name typed just to the right of "attention to" on the front.

Beuregard opened the envelope, thinking it might be some type of solicitation, or worse yet, a prank. But his interest was piqued considerably when he removed the sheet of paper from inside and scanned the bizarre-looking type on the unfolded page.

After he'd read the first paragraph, his eyes widened in anticipation. It was clear that this was something that warranted further investigation. He read the following:

Dear Chicago Police,

Let me start by commending you officers on the wonderful job you do every day, putting your lives on the line to protect the citizens of this great city. What courage you guys must have to go into some of those dangerous and shitty neighborhoods, right? I certainly couldn't do it. So my hat's off to you, gentlemen! Bravo for a job well done!

It's been widely reported in the news that crime in the city is down. C'mon, is it really? That's hard to tell with all of the shootings and murders taking place. And I bet it's a lot worse than what you guys are letting on. You're not fooling me. Ha! Not to worry, though. Everything isn't going to make the news. I'm sure the Chicago PD will see to it.

I imagine that with all of your experience and knowhow, not to mention the latest CSI type of technology you guys have at your disposal, you assume you know who is behind the murders of Taylor Hagenstock and Samantha Collier. But nothing could be further from the truth. Because, you see, I'm not who you think I am. I wasn't born yesterday, and I certainly ain't stupid!

I sit in my comfy living room and watch you guys on TV, pathetically trying your best to explain to the public why you haven't been able to solve these murders. It's fucking hilarious, to tell you the truth! I bet the mayor has his foot pretty far up your asses, not to mention that election

time is coming around. We certainly can't
have murders downtown, now, can we?

Well, I think I've said enough for now.
Just so you know, I won't stop until I
reach my ultimate goal. If you guys can
figure that out, you'll have my utmost
respect! But, hey, don't count on it,
fucking LOSERS!

Cheers, 404

After finishing, Beuregard thought for a moment. "The nerve of this son of a bitch," he muttered. "He's taunting us." Beuregard bolted out of his office and hurried catty-corner to the office of his boss, Chief of Detectives Chuck Kirkendall, to show him the letter.

"You busy?"

"Nah, what's up?"

"I just got this letter in the mail. Whoever this moron is, he's claiming responsibility for the Hagenstock and Collier murders. Take a look."

Beuregard handed the letter to Kirkendall, who leaned back in his office chair, took in a deep breath and read it, examining every word in minute detail. Once he was finished, he removed his glasses and leaned toward his desk.

"Well, I'll be. You need to get this to forensics and see if they can get some DNA off of it, other than our prints, of course. This guy's got some balls, I'll say."

"He signed off with the number 404. What the hell does that mean?"

"I don't know, but it must have some type of significance, either to himself or these cases in general."

"When I read this pathetic ass's excuse for humor, one thing stood out to me. He mentions that he's not who we think he is. You catch that?"

"Yeah, I did. Is he sayin' that we're not on the right path, or what?"

"Not sure. He may be trying to throw us off the track. Psychopaths like this seem to think they're so fucking much smarter than everyone else."

"If we can get a DNA match from this envelope to what we were able to recover from the bodies of both women, bingo. We can link this asshole to the crime and show him just how smart he is."

Preston Ponder, a highly acclaimed FBI Special Agent who was in town for another case, suddenly walked by, quickly getting the attention of both cops.

"Ponder, you got a minute?" Beuregard asked.

Ponder, wearing a black, tailored Italian suit and gleaming black loafers, stopped in the office to talk to both officers.

"Gentlemen, what's going on?" he said as he extended his hand for a shake.

"You familiar with the Hagenstock case? The unsolved murder we got downtown?"

"How couldn't I be? It's been all over the news," Ponder said.

"This letter came today in the mail. We think it might be from the perp, claiming responsibility. Take a look, and tell us what you make of it," Beuregard said.

Ponder grabbed a handkerchief from his pocket and used it to take the letter from Beuregard so he could begin reading. When he was finished, he looked at both Beuregard and Kirkendall.

"We're trying to figure out what the signoff with '404' means," Kirkendall said.

"The first thing that comes to my mind is the web page error message."

"What do you mean?"

"You guys are that clueless? I thought you were computer savvy. '404' is an error message displayed when a page on the internet can't be found, or is considered unknown."

Beuregard and Kirkendall looked at each other, then back at Ponder.

"So perhaps, and I'm just guessing here, he signed off as 404 because his identity, as far as you guys are concerned, is unknown."

Beuregard shrugged and looked sheepishly at Kirkendall. "Now, why the hell didn't we know that?"

"Your guess is as good as mine." Ponder went on, "The fact that this guy is mentioning that he's not who we think he is leads me to believe that he's being deceptive somehow. In what way, I'm not sure."

"I'd love to nail this son of a bitch myself, so I could personally deliver him to the families of both of these women," said Beuregard.

"Not to burst your bubble here, but I've seen cases like this where these scumbags go to great lengths to conceal their identity. If you guys can get me as many details as possible, I'll have a profile analysis done to help us get closer to nabbing this sleazeball. The Bureau's regional forensics lab is right here downtown, of course. So, what's the verdict?"

Kirkendall reared back in his office chair, putting his hands behind his head, glaring firmly at Ponder. "You got it," he said.

Beuregard said, "Good looking out, Ponder. I knew you Feds were good for something besides pushing pencils. Now, I imagine with you involved, if we can solve this damn thing, it'd be of a lot of help toward us avoiding the mayor's wrath!"

CHAPTER **10**

DETECTIVE HOWARD BEUREGARD calmly walked through the corridor of Chicago's 1st District station holding a freshly made cup of Starbuck's, angling toward a holding cell.

"Dr. Fields, today is your lucky day, sweetheart. You've been cleared of any pending charges, for now."

"What is that supposed to mean?"

"Exactly how it sounds. So far, your alibi's checked out and we were able to confirm with the hospital that you were indeed on duty the evening Taylor Hagenstock was murdered. However, there are still some issues that need to be addressed, just not out of necessity to keep you in custody."

"I wish you guys had listened to me when you first arrested me."

"We still have to do our jobs, which brings me to the next issue. I'd like for you to hold tight for a minute. I have someone who would like to ask you a few questions. Is that okay?"

"Sure. You guys have caused me to be off work for several days, not to mention the embarrassment. I guess another hour or two of sitting here wouldn't hurt."

"All right, good. Follow me back. We're having a little boardroom meeting down the hall."

Alexis walked with Beuregard into a small conference room where they were accompanied by another detective and FBI Special Agent Preston Ponder.

"Dr. Alexis Fields, I'd like you to meet Preston Ponder, one of the FBI's finest special agents, and CPD Detective First Class Stephen Wiggans."

Alexis stared at the incredibly handsome Ponder as if she'd just been introduced to a famous celebrity. Cops and FBI agents weren't supposed to look this good or dress this stylishly, she thought.

"Dr. Fields, it's a pleasure to meet you," Ponder said, extending his hand.

"Likewise," Wiggans added.

"You're the young lady who was involved in the case up in Lake Park, Illinois. The vacant house used as a drug hub by the rogue cop ring, El Subida. I remembered seeing your name in the case report," Ponder said.

Alexis nodded, then answered curtly, "That was yours truly. Trouble seems to follow me wherever I go."

"I've been briefed on what's happened here, both with the murders of the two women downtown as well as your arrest. And I want to help. Not only the Chicago police, but you as well."

"So, what exactly do you need from me?"

"For starters, I'd like for you to tell me some basic history about you and your ex-boyfriend. His name is Wilfred Bachman, is that correct?"

"Yes."

"According to an interdepartmental memo and BOLO, he's been seen in the area. Were you aware of that?"

"I was told, and figured as much. When I was living in Madison with my mother, I was involved with him. We were supposed to get married. That was our plan. It's what I was looking forward to initially, before I decided to end the relationship."

"What changed?"

Alexis ran her fingers through her hair, took in a breath and swallowed hard. "He had lost his job, and suddenly became this withdrawn, irritable and possessive character. It was like I didn't know him anymore, who he was, or what he was capable of. But things really took a turn for the worse the night I officially broke up with him. He grabbed me in front of my house. I struggled to get away from him. Then he put a knife to my throat."

"And according to the information I have, the police have been looking for him ever since the incident, also wanting to talk to him as a person of interest about a murder in Madison," said Ponder.

"That's true. A neighbor who lived across the street from my mother and I intervened, scaring Wilfred off. His name was Bill Finnegan, but everyone on the block called him Vietnam Billy, because he was a war veteran. As Wilfred retreated to his SUV, he glared at Bill and me with this menacing look, and threatened revenge, remarking that 'it's not over.'"

"And you were recently attacked in your home by an intruder, found unconscious in the parking garage of your condominium building and taken to the hospital. Is that correct?"

"That's correct. I believed it was him. But I couldn't be one hundred percent sure. I think in Wilfred's current state of mind, he's certainly capable of doing something like that. Whoever it was that night had a mask on. I couldn't see his face, didn't recognize his voice. And I have absolutely no idea how he got into my place."

"Well, with the cooperation of the Chicago PD, I've been able to uncover some interesting facts we'd like to share with you. For starters, our forensics team was able to trace the IP address of the computer used to converse with Taylor Hagenstock the night of her death. This would mean that someone had to actively be using the computer in question between 7:00 p.m. and 7:40 p.m."

"Detective Beuregard has already acknowledged that I was at work that evening. I work nights most of the time in the ER. I'm not crazy about it, but I knew that would be my schedule the day I was hired."

"I'm fully aware of that. But what's puzzling to me is that even though your name and address could have been used falsely, the IP address, meaning the computer footprint that forensics has identified, traces back to your physical address and to your PC specifically. It could be, if it was him who attacked you that night, that he may have access to your condo and in turn to your computer as well. If I were you, the first thing I'd do when I returned home is have my locks changed."

"I'll do that right away."

"You live on the first floor?"

"No, I live on the fifth floor. I was adamant about not being on the first floor, if, for no other reason but this."

"So, a would-be assailant being able to climb through your window is highly unlikely?"

"No way could someone do it. I think it's extremely unlikely. Even with a ladder."

"Okay. Well, I've been saving the most interesting stuff for last. CPD obtained some video from several nearby businesses. These are some screenshots from the footage. They're a little blurry, but we can make out some important details here."

After taking various black and white photographs from a manila envelope, Ponder handed the pictures to Alexis to examine. He then leaned over, pointing to the hazy figures in the glossy prints.

"This picture is critical. In this frame you'll see what looks like two women walking down Wells Street as they leave the restaurant. Here's another. As they turn toward the parking garage, one of the underground security cameras snapped a close-up of the person alleged to be Sarah Stalworth."

"I don't know how much of that is bad photo quality, but she looks hideous!" Alexis said.

"I agree, and it's something that one of the waitresses from the Big Bowl corroborated when we interviewed her. She was the one who served them, and said that at first she suspected Stalworth of being transgender. But as the night rolled on, she became less sure."

"So how does this tie in with everything else?"

"Keep following me, here." Ponder received another package from Wiggans and quickly unsealed the envelope. "Now, take a look at these photos. These were taken inside the vestibule of Samantha Collier's apartment building the night she was murdered. Do you see the similarities?"

"I do. To me it looks like the same person." Alexis paused for a tense moment. "But I still don't understand how this all ties together."

"During the autopsy on Hagenstock's body, forensics found semen inside of her vagina. It was concluded that someone had intercourse with her during the night she was murdered, either before she was killed or a short while after. There was also internal bruising and some vaginal tearing, a good indication that the act was not consensual."

"How gross for any woman to go through that trauma. Believe me, I know firsthand. It's awful!"

"It most certainly is," Ponder said, and nodded. "I say all this to make an interesting point, that maybe, just maybe, Wilfred Bachman has been meandering around committing these murders while pretending to be a woman."

Alexis shook her head. "Unbelievable. If that's true, I would have never suspected him to be capable of it."

"Have you ever known him to hint around that he'd enjoy dressing as a woman?"

"Absolutely not. I would have ended it a long time ago if I'd ever seen that, or even thought that he might be hiding that type of fetish. Then again, nothing much surprises me any more."

"We've requested that a profile be done by supervisory special agents in the FBI's Behavioral Science Unit, giving them pertinent details about what we've been able to put together thus far. Nothing was left on the table as far as analysis goes. Their conclusion, based on the evidence presented, was that it is very possible, and even likely, that Bachman could reach this level of deportment."

Alexis frowned at Ponder, feeling confused, and said, "I really find all of this troubling, especially given the fact that this is someone I was not only romantically involved with, but whom I was considering spending the rest of my life with."

"I know it's hard to fathom. But men like this can be incredibly persuasive, even charming, with good intentions on the surface, all while hiding their ulterior motives."

"He's a smart but scary person," Alexis said.

"What kind of work does he do? Does he have any kind of special interests, hobbies or skills that you're aware of?"

"He's a computer whiz. A programmer. He's always tinkered with computers, putting them together, that sort of thing. He had aspirations of one day starting his own consulting company. But his interests waned once he'd lost his job and could no longer find employment."

"You mean his interest in starting a company, or computers in general?"

"Definitely in starting a company. He went into survival mode, complaining about money he'd spent on me in the past. He started blaming everyone else for his problems: the president, politicians, the right-wing conservatives. And he became increasingly paranoid, jealous and extremely possessive."

Ponder paused and looked at the other cops in the room. "His proficiency and background with computers could explain the 404 response code he signed off the letter with."

"What do you mean?" Alexis asked.

"Beuregard received an anonymous letter in the mail taunting the Chicago police about both murders. Whoever wrote it claimed that he's not who we think he is, and ended the letter with the numbers 404, which is an internet error message for 'page unknown or can't be found'."

"This is getting stranger by the minute," Alexis said curtly.

"I don't want to alarm you, Dr. Fields, but the reality is, your life may be in grave danger unless we can get to him first. He's seemed to become increasingly psychotic in his behavior. I would also suggest that you increase your means of personal security, including around your home."

CHAPTER 11

AS I SAT in this less-than-friendly, utilitarian-looking police room, staring at these men briefly huddled, talking among themselves, there was a brisk knock on the door.

Ushered inside was a middle-aged, somberly looking couple. The woman's face was battle-weary, her hair mostly black with some streaks of gray.

"Dr. Fields, we'd like for you to meet Travis and Donna Hagenstock, parents of Taylor Hagenstock."

"Pleased to meet you," I said, extending a warm handshake to them both. I couldn't begin to imagine the pain they were feeling. It was all too evident on their faces.

There was momentary silence in the room, as if the world itself had suddenly come to an inexplicable halt.

"I'm so sorry for the loss of your daughter," I added.

"Thank you," Mrs. Hagenstock said.

"Our meeting with Dr. Fields here ran over. I hope you don't mind the extra company," Beuregard said to the Hagenstocks.

"No. We're fine with it, Detective."

"I'd like to thank you both for coming down to talk to us today, and want you to know that we've made some good progress in possibly finding out who killed your daughter. It's a top priority, not only for me but for my colleagues as well."

"We appreciate your efforts as well as theirs, Mr. Beuregard. Taylor was our only child and she meant the world to us. Whoever committed this despicable act not only snatched our daughter away from us, they destroyed a part of us, too."

"I understand completely," Beuregard replied.

"I might add that we're not the type of parents who will stand before the world and pretend their child was perfect. She certainly had her flaws, as most do. But to us, she was as perfect as could be."

Travis Hagenstock went into the pocket of his car coat and retrieved a folded piece of paper, then handed it to Beuregard.

"That being said, we found something in her room recently that we thought could be helpful in your investigation."

"Okay." Beuregard took the paper, unfolded it and scanned it.

"Taylor was very organized, very detailed, and always kept an envelope of receipts for her purchases. In the top drawer of the dresser in her bedroom there was an invoice from a web designer she'd paid to have a blog designed. My wife and I were quite surprised when we found it. We'd had no idea she was a blogger. She'd never mentioned it. Why, we don't know. Here is a copy, with the name of the blog, the web designer's name, and a description of the services rendered. We'd like for you to keep it, to use as one more piece of potential evidence in finding her killer."

"I appreciate your willingness to come forward with this information. Anything we can get our hands on like this could be crucial to the investigation."

"There's one other thing. I'm sure you've heard by now, Detective, and neither my wife nor I ever had any qualms about it."

"Yes?"

"Our daughter Taylor was gay. We first had our suspicions when she was a teenager. Once she'd gone away to college, she came out and confided in us that this was who she was. She'd even had a lover at one point whom she seemed quite enamored with. We always loved her for who she was, no matter what. She respected us, and our relationship with her was better for it."

As I listened to these grief-stricken people pour their hearts and souls out to these men they hardly knew, I thought about my own parents, and the deep-seated bond I shared with my beloved mother.

My father had never been an integral part of my life. He'd left my mother and I when I was three years old for what he referred to as a "quest to find himself." The pain of growing up with him selfishly absent had undeniably affected me in countless ways.

I didn't even know whether my father was alive or dead. No one I knew, knew for sure. Could that be the reason why I had such a hard time with men? Could I be some type of magnet for psychopaths and their penchant for wanting to harm me?

The same thug who had brutally taken the lives of these two women was still at large, slowly slinking toward his or her next victim, and I could be that hapless target, caught in the crosshairs.

As my heart thudded in my chest, I realized that there was one thing I could declare, and that I knew for sure. I was a survivor. I was strong.

I was determined to get through this.

CHAPTER 12

"I NEED TO buy a gun. You know where I could get one?" I asked Jasten Weir, whom I'd run into after a mandatory conference at work.

"Alexis, what the hell do you need a gun for? You plan on shooting someone?"

"I need it for protection, without going into a lot of detail. Do you know of anyone?"

"I do. I do. Before I became a nurse practitioner, I used to hang around with some shady characters, believe it or not. My parents didn't approve of the association and quickly sent me off to med school in another state. So, here I am. Anyway, why don't you go through the process? You know Chicago's got that concealed carry thing going on now."

"I don't have time for that. I need one like yesterday."

Weir's expression turned glum. "Shit. I take it you're in a serious fix. Listen, here's what I'll do. I know a guy who lives on the South Side. I used to run with him back home in Miami. He straightened up his life and moved here about a year ago to be with his girlfriend. He might be able to help us out here."

"I'll only buy it if it's clean, free of any illegal history."

"Okay, I'll emphasize that when I talk to him."

"Thank you, Jasten. And don't tell anyone about this!"

"I won't. You mind telling me what you need it for?"

"It's for my own protection. That's all I can tell you right now. There's some crazy people out there. Living here in Chicago, I'm sure you see it every day."

"Without a doubt. And I know you see a lot of it being in the ER. By the way, I'll walk you to your car if you want me to. It's the least I can do, since I can't get you to go out with me," Jasten said, and smiled.

"Wow, you are persistent, aren't you? I'll have to at least give you an A for effort. Besides, your plate's full already," I shot back.

As Jasten and I walked toward the employee parking lot of the hospital, I felt as if someone was covertly watching us. I looked around as we meandered through several rows of cars and SUVs before we arrived at the section where my BMW was parked.

"Alexis, are you, like, in imminent danger right now? You're so uptight and jittery."

"Listen, Jasten," I said as we walked, looking behind us and over my shoulder. "I have a crazy ex who's trying to harm me. I have a restraining order out against him. That's the reason why I need the gun."

"Oh, I understand completely now. You can't take things like that lightly. I literally hate watching the news these days. These bullshit cases of losers killing their wives and girlfriends are everywhere. So, listen, as a friend, anytime you need to be escorted in and out of the building, if I'm here and available, I'll walk with you."

"That's very sweet of you. Do you remember when I was in the hospital as a patient several weeks ago?"

"Yeah, the rumor that floated around was that you had some type of accident and injured yourself."

"The truth is, I *was* injured. But it was no accident. I was physically assaulted in my condo by an attacker. To this day, I have no idea who the hell it was."

"Shit, I'm sorry. I didn't know."

"He got away. Stopped when he saw one of the other residents running to their car in the parking garage, I was told. If it wasn't for that person's intervention, I might be dead right now."

"So, you think it was your ex?"

"I can't say for sure. The asshole wore a mask. He damn near killed me that night. I suffered a serious head injury, and I'm still not sure if I'm completely okay."

"If I were you I'd alert hospital security. They could provide extra protection for you."

"I really don't want to do that. I don't want them digging around in my personal life."

We had almost made it to my X5 when a homeless man with white hair and a mangy beard, wearing tattered clothes, suddenly appeared from between two parked cars, just to the right of my SUV.

"Can I appeal to either of you honorable souls to help me get something to eat?" he asked in a raspy baritone.

I reached into my purse to give him a couple of dollars as Jasten looked on. "Here. That's all the change I have. I hope that helps you," I said, laying the crisp bills in his hand.

He nodded and gave me a look of concern. "Your eyes give way to the discernment of your woes," he suddenly said.

"Excuse me? What did you say?" I replied.

He shrugged and then smiled. "I mean you only goodwill. It is my gift, young lady. Which to me is reprehensible if not shared. Close are your friends, but even closer are your enemies," he went on.

I nodded with appreciation. "Thank you kindly," I responded, peering at him curiously as he turned and hobbled away.

Jasten shrugged, then turned to me and said, "God knows what that guy was talking about. Alexis, if you need me to follow you home, I'd be willing. It's no problem."

I didn't know whether Jasten was sincerely looking out for my best interests, or if he thought there was a possibility for some sort of love connection this evening. But something told me to take him up on his offer.

"Okay, if you're offering, I live ten minutes away."

He smiled, opened the door to my car so I could climb in, and told me that he'd run to his car and follow me home.

I put my key in the ignition, started the car, and slowly backed out of my reserved parking space. Jasten whirled around the corner, following me out of the parking lot onto State Street.

It's not safe here, I kept telling myself. And how the hell had that panhandler slipped past hospital security and into employee parking?

Jasten followed me into the parking garage of my condo building. I had to give him credit for acting like a perfect gentleman, which was more than I could say for most men I'd met in the Windy City.

Jasten and I parked our vehicles and entered the underground foyer. He gawked as we passed several blondes in spandex working out at the building's private fitness center.

"Snazzy place. You been here long?" he asked as we walked through the corridor to the elevator.

"Ever since I came to Chicago. I had a house in Lake Park before that. That's a whole other story in itself."

"Don't tell me you had lowlifes chasing you there too?" he said.

I had to chuckle, even though it was no laughing matter. Jasten reminded me of the inquisitive little brother I'd never had, always asking questions.

"You wouldn't believe me if I told you," I quipped.

"Try me," he said.

"Okay, I bought a house and lived there while I worked at Veterans Memorial Hospital for my internship. There was a supposedly vacant house next door to me. At night, suspicious-looking men kept going in and out. Horrified at what I saw, I called the police, and after that my life was never the same."

"What happened, exactly?" Jasten inquired as we approached my door.

"Some of the police I encountered were wickedly brazen and corrupt, and saw me as a threat to a vicious crime ring they'd established. They used the house next door as a central point in their operation, which included a facility beneath it for transporting illegal weapons and drugs in and out of the city, and to hide women and girls caught up in the sex trade."

"Now, that's insane! Who'd imagine the police being that deep into it like that? I'm glad you're okay."

"Well, that remains to be seen. I've still got a psychopath of an ex on the loose who might be in Chicago as we speak."

I unlocked the dead bolt and bottom lock, then Jasten and I walked into my condo. Inside, the room was as black as a wormhole in space, but before I could flip the switch to turn on the lights, Jasten blurted something that startled me.

"You have a beam of light coming through the center of your wall, over the couch."

"What? What do you mean?"

"Leave the lights off. Come here and look," he said.

He grabbed my hand, guiding me toward him as he showed me the light filtering into my living room from the condo unit next door. Was this just a hole from a missing nail? A construction defect? Or something appallingly worse?

"I'll look closer," Jasten said.

"You know what, don't bother," I said. "I remember hearing some new tenants moving in about a week ago, and I don't want to invade their privacy," I said.

"You sure?"

"Yeah, I'm sure. I heard them moving furniture, and hammering. They probably inadvertently poked that hole in the wall somehow. Despite how pretty it looks, this building doesn't have what you'd call bang-up construction. I'll contact management and have them send someone to patch it up. It's no big deal."

Jasten turned toward me and said, "Now, what would you do without me?"

"I have no idea," I said with a smirk. "But thank you for being so observant. I knew there was a good reason I had you follow me home!"

CHAPTER 13

Go get 'em Terrell!

I WATCHED AS ominous gray clouds tracked over Rockne Stadium, the brisk Chicago wind sparring with and daring several thousand enthusiastic, screaming fans and supporters to clutch their hats and umbrellas.

The stadium scoreboard read two minutes and twelve seconds to go in the fourth quarter. My young friend Terrell's team, the Dolphins, was up by seven, and the opposing team had the ball on their own forty-two yard line.

On the next play, a third down, the quarterback threw a long pass over the middle of the field, the ball was tipped by the receiver, and Terrell made what looked to be an amazing, game-winning interception.

"Wow! What a play!" I thought as I watched. I had never been a big fan of the Badgers at UW, nor did I ever watch the Packers play, but I knew my way around the game. I was thrilled for Terrell, and glad that I could keep my promise by attending one of his games.

I waited around with parents and faculty after it was over. I wanted to make sure that Terrell saw me, to personally congratulate him on the victory. Suddenly, Terrell and his parents came trudging out of the visitors' locker room.

"Great game, Terrell!" I beamed.

"Thanks, Ms. Alex."

I extended my arm to shake his parents' hands. "Hi, I'm Alexis Fields. I live in the same condominium complex that you do, on the fifth floor, and know Terrell from seeing him in the building," I said.

"Pleased to meet you," Terrell's father said. "I'm Tobias, and this here is my lovely wife Yolanda."

"I'm sure you must be very proud of him. He's such a good kid," I said.

"We are. Absolutely. And we're glad that he's able to participate in athletics *and* keep up an excellent grade point average at the same time."

As I smiled and looked at Terrell with approval, my cell suddenly buzzed in my purse. "Excuse me," I told the Burtons. "I need to take this."

I stepped several feet away and grabbed my new iPhone to look at the display window. I stared in terror as I read the glowing text:

"HOPE YOU LIKED THE GAME. IT WILL BE THE LAST YOU'LL EVER SEE!" the words read.

I swallowed hard. I didn't recognize the number or know who could have sent the text. Whomever it had come from, the text meant two terrifying things: that someone nefarious had my new cell number, and they were watching my every move.

I turned toward the Burton family with a solemn and flushed look on my face.

"Is everything okay?" Judge Burton asked.

"Sure. I… I'd better be going. It's an urgent matter. It was nice meeting you both. Congratulations on your win, Terrell," I said nervously.

I spun on my heel, quickly trudged past vendors selling game souvenirs, and exited the field area to slip through the parking lot.

My heart began pounding in my chest. I thought about the murders of Taylor Hagenstock and Samantha Collier, and wondered if Wilfred was somehow involved. If so, was I next on the list?

I grabbed my X5's key fob from my purse, remotely unlocking the vehicle as I approached it. After I had cranked the engine and backed out of my parking space, my cell phone buzzed again. I glanced at it once more, petrified, and was surprised to see that it was Detective Beuregard from Chicago PD calling.

"Dr. Fields?" he asked.

"Yes?"

"Beuregard here from CPD. Listen, we've been talking to some detectives in Madison and Lake Park, and we have even more reason to believe you're in danger. Bachman has been withdrawing money with his mother's debit card, with transactions showing as recently as yesterday from an ATM in Chicago."

My heart once again began beating aggressively. I could feel my blood pressure rise.

"Thank God you've called, Detective! I was going to call you as well. Actually, I've just received a text that scared the hell out of me. I believe it could be from him."

"What did it say?"

"It said, 'Hope you liked the game. It will be the last you ever see.' I'd just come from a high school football game. A kid I know in my building was playing. So, whoever knew I was there is obviously watching me."

"Do you have someone who can accompany you while you're at home?"

"It's only me. I could always have my mom or a friend stay with me temporarily."

"That wouldn't be a bad idea. Not at all. And neither would arming yourself. You own a gun?"

"Not at the moment. But, trust me, it's something I'm working on."

"Good. So, where are you now?"

"I'm currently heading East on Madison Ave."

"All right. Just a little FYI—watch your surroundings. Be safe. Chicago can be a very dangerous city, especially in certain areas. You have my cell number if you need me. In an extreme emergency, just call 911 and then call me afterwards. Patrol units in the area can get to you a lot quicker than I can."

"Okay. I appreciate it, Detective."

After ending the call, I scanned the area immediately surrounding my X5 each and every time I stopped at a traffic light. Darkness had begun to envelop the city on a day that had already been mostly overcast.

Once I'd arrived home, I quickly exited my vehicle and ran across the ground level of the parking garage to enter the building. After leaving the elevator, I felt a sense of relief as I approached the door to enter my condo.

I walked inside, dropped my purse on the kitchen table and looked in the refrigerator. Dammit! No leftovers. There was nothing I could heat up for dinner, and I was certainly not up to venturing out again. Not tonight.

A nice hot shower sounded like a good plan, so I went into my bathroom, moved the shower curtain sideways, and leaned over to turn on the shower. Then I noticed something strange.

Sitting on the top of my pedestal sink was a folded piece of paper. It appeared to be a newspaper clipping.

My hands shook as I picked up the article and unfolded it to see what it said.

I didn't remember leaving it there. What the hell was this? As I unfolded it, my eyes widened with fear at the headline staring back at me:

DOCTOR NARROWLY SURVIVES MURDER ATTEMPT BY COP, HELPS TAKE DOWN ROGUE COP RING

My lips trembled. Tears streamed down my cheeks. *Oh, God, no, please don't let this be true!* I had never imagined my whole life turning into a horrible nightmare. But here I was, gripped in a panic that was as real as life itself.

The article seemed to be a warning about Mike Crowley, the sick son of a bitch I'd emptied that gun into. The monster of a cop who had sexually assaulted me, then tried to kill my friend John Hill and me, but instead got what he deserved in the crash of Hill's Ford Fusion after it had gone veering over the cliff and into the ravine that night.

How in hell had this gotten here? What the hell had my life turned into?

This wasn't some spooky tale being told to kids around a campfire at night. This was terror in the making, featuring none other than yours truly.

I quickly snapped off the running water and darted out of the bathroom, grabbing my purse as I dashed for the front door. As I opened it to leave, only one thought had crossed my mind.

The real nightmare has just begun.

And I need to go!

CHAPTER **14**

AS LONG AS it was in motion, my SUV was the only place I felt safe. Someone had obviously been in my home again. This time, it almost seemed as if it were someone other than Wilfred. How could that be? And why?

I called my mother, not wanting to alarm her, but to ask her if she'd been in touch with Lou Haney, the detective who had been working my case against Wilfred in Madison, and to see how she was doing.

After hearing her voicemail greeting, I left a message in a quivering voice for her to call me. My heart still in a panic, I drove around Chicago, wondering what my next move would be in this chess game of terror.

I considered moving from my condo to an undisclosed location. *Take a loss on it and just sell the damn thing, already!* I told myself. Nothing was more important than my life right now.

It was getting late. I'd had no sleep and was scheduled to be at work at 5 a.m.

After I'd meandered through downtown Chicago for a while, I pulled in front of the Hyatt Regency and quickly turned in to the parking area to hand my keys to the valet.

I'd decided to stay here for several days, to clear my head, and for my own safety.

I walked through the lobby, straight toward the cream-colored granite check-in desk.

"May I help you?" asked the smiling clerk, taking in my serious demeanor and now shiny, wet eyes.

"Yes, I need a room for the night. It doesn't matter what size. Whatever you have available," I said.

The clerk looked at his list of vacancies. "Ah, we do have something available. How long would you be staying?"

"Several days, at least. I'll have to play it by ear. And I need a wake up-call for 3:30 a.m. this morning. Here's my credit card."

"Absolutely, we can accommodate you. It'll take just a minute to process this, and I'll have your room key ready," he said.

The only thing I wanted at this moment was to climb into bed without looking over my shoulder.

I would have plenty of reasons to do just that during the next several days.

CHAPTER 15

AFTER I LEFT the hospital, I peeled out of employee parking in my SUV in a manic state of desperation. It was imperative I talk to Special Agent Preston Ponder, especially after finding the news article in my condo. He was the only one who had a connection to what had happened in Lake Park, and to what had transpired in Chicago.

I hightailed it over to the 1st District station, the only place where I had a chance in hell of finding him. I pulled up to the front of the building, paid for my parking space, and quickly entered, walking past several cops standing outside.

As I stepped inside, confronting me was a bulldog of a woman who looked at me with an expression somewhere between annoyance and resentment. "Yes? What can we do for you?" she growled.

"I'm looking for an FBI agent, Preston Ponder. Is he here?"

"Do you have an appointment to see him?"

"No, I don't. But it's urgent. Can you get him and tell him it's Dr. Alexis Fields, please?"

"Well, I don't know if he's going to see you without an appointment. Couldn't you call first? What does this concern, anyway?"

My patience was wearing thin. I didn't have time for a face-off. What the hell was this woman trying to prove, anyway? Win a pissing contest? I made a dash toward the hallway, asking other uniformed officers standing nearby, "Is Preston Ponder here? Does anyone know if he's here right now?"

The rude cow then stood up and walked around her desk, coming after me vigorously. "Hold her! She's trying to go upstairs," she barked.

"Listen, it's imperative that I see Preston Ponder, the FBI agent," I demanded of the male officers standing in front of me.

In the meantime, someone must have contacted him and told him I was downstairs, that a crazy woman was here to see him. Once I saw him step off the elevator, walking toward me, I immediately regained my composure and calmed down.

"Dr. Fields. So we meet again. I'm told you were asking for me."

"Agent Ponder, if you have time, I really need to talk to you. It's urgent," I said.

"Sure enough. Let's head up to my office and talk."

We started down the corridor. Glancing around, I could see that I was the subject of some leering, not-too-nice conversations. I imagined that a flurry of four letter words was happening as well. We stepped into the elevator, then awkwardly waited until it reached the third floor.

"I'll be in Chicago working on your case, as well as another, for the foreseeable future," he said. "Please, come this way."

We walked down another corridor into a large office space with cubicles, glass partitions and several curious onlookers. I felt like an extra on the set of one of those gritty, Chicago-based cop shows.

"Have a seat," he said and motioned to a chair as he looped around and took the chair behind his desk. "What brings you in today?"

I reached into my purse and nervously pulled out the newspaper article. "I have this," I said. "I found it in my condo, on the bathroom sink. I have no idea how it got there."

Ponder looked at the page. I could see that it instantly became evident to him that there was some type of link to what had happened in Lake Park.

"Have you told CPD about this?" he asked.

"No, I haven't. I've told them everything else. But this time I wanted to speak to you directly. Because of your familiarity with the case in Lake Park, I felt you'd already be aware of the connection."

"Did you ever have your locks changed? Are you still staying at your condo?"

"I'm still there for the time being. But I've stayed at the Hyatt Regency the last several nights. And yes, I've had my locks changed, but somehow, apparently, someone still got this in there. And I don't know what to make of it."

"Does anyone else have access to your unit? Perhaps a maintenance person? Building manager?"

"I believe our management office has access to our units in case of an emergency. Even so, they're supposed to notify us if they need access."

Ponder leaned forward, his eyes holding mine. "I've got some ideas. Give me a few days. I need to sit down and clear this not only with my superiors, but with CPD's top brass too. I'd like to meet with you at your home, which will play a part in this as well. In the meantime, it's important that your day-to-day routine remain unchanged. Don't be alarmed. I'll explain everything, and it should all make sense to you when I do."

"Whatever you say. Just tell me what to do."

CHAPTER **16**

HOWARD BEUREGARD'S VAST experience assured him that deciphering more clues and finding the now infamous "404 Killer" were imperative before the two cases grew cold.

He quickly opened the top drawer of his desk and pulled out the case file and the invoice he'd been given by the parents of Taylor Hagenstock, then carefully studied the payment receipt for the creation of her blog.

Her web pages had been deleted from the hosting company's servers after her untimely death. However, Beuregard was given access to stored backup files and received printed copies, in chronological order, just as the posts had been published by Hagenstock.

As he reviewed hundreds of blog posts, spanning approximately eighteen months, nothing seemed to be out of the ordinary. On the surface, the posts read like ordinary "girl talk" from a young woman who wanted to chronicle her life's daily activities—until Beuregard got to the last page.

The blog post read:

"Sometimes in life we dare to go beyond our comfort zone and chart new territory. We endure the unknown, bravely, to see what may lie ahead, which will change our lives for the better. That being said, I'm overjoyed to announce that I'm pregnant with my very first child!"

"Shit, she was pregnant?" Beuregard muttered. He took a deep breath. *Pregnant. By whom?* he wondered. There had been no reason for the coroner to check to see if Hagenstock had been pregnant when she was murdered. But such a harrowing revelation added a new dimension to where Chicago Police and the FBI would go from here.

Beuregard laid the sheet of paper on his desk and picked up the phone to schedule a meeting for the difficult task of telling Hagenstock's parents about the pregnancy.

"I need to talk to you and your husband. It's urgent. I can be there in fifteen or twenty minutes," he blurted when Donna Hagenstock answered the phone.

Beuregard ended the call, grabbed his jacket and briskly walked downstairs to climb into his black, unmarked police vehicle. The Hagenstocks lived in suburban Oak Park. He headed onto the Eisenhower Expressway, merging with lunch-hour traffic, and promptly arrived at their white Cape Cod on a quiet, tree-lined strip within twenty-two minutes.

When Beuregard walked in, the first thing he noticed was Donna Hagenstock's eyes, which were bloodshot and sporting dark circles underneath, undoubtedly from crying and lack of sleep. The Hagenstocks looked concerned but hopeful that he had some sort of good news to share.

Perhaps a revelation.

The three anxiously sat down in the living room, eager to get started.

"Mrs. Hagenstock," Beuregard said, "did you have any knowledge of your daughter having a relationship with a man?"

"No, only with women. Why do you ask, Detective?"

"There's no easy way to put this. But on August 17th she announced to the world via her blog that she was pregnant."

The Hagenstocks looked perplexed.

"Are you sure?" Mrs. Hagenstock asked. "I mean, how can you be sure? Couldn't she have posted it as a prank? It wouldn't be the first time that she clowned around in public."

"I understand your skepticism and need for closure. And I'll be a hundred percent sure when the autopsy results are completed. But I don't want to wait, losing precious time by not following up on this lead.

Whoever this guy is, he's trying to stay one step ahead of us." Beuregard's eyes narrowed to a squint. "With all due respect, Mr. and Mrs. Hagenstock, time is of the essence here in finding your daughter's killer."

Mrs. Hagenstock angled her gaze out the front picture window of their living room.

"Travis and I would have been utterly thrilled with the idea of having a grandchild. Although we would have preferred it happen during marriage. We completely understand the times in which we live." She took a nervous breath as tears tracked down her cheeks. "Why on earth would she keep something important like that from us?"

"Maybe she was going to tell you, but hadn't yet found the courage," Beuregard said.

Mrs. Hagenstock daintily wiped her eyes with a tissue, then looked up at Beuregard, who was standing now. She said, "Please find whoever did this, Detective. You've got to find him, not only for Taylor, but to prevent someone else from going through the same pain and suffering that's gutted us from the inside."

"We will. And we won't stop until we do. But I need more information. Did she have any friends I could talk to who may know more about what was going on in her personal life?"

"She had one special friend that I recall. Michelle Darcy. Her family moved out of the neighborhood some years ago, but she and Taylor still kept in touch. They were close."

"Do you have her phone number? Possibly an email address?"

"I believe so. We invited Michelle and her parents to our twenty-fifth wedding anniversary dinner party several years ago. Let me find her information for you."

Mrs. Hagenstock went to her bedroom and retrieved the phone number, handing it to Beuregard on a folded white piece of paper.

Beuregard said, "I'll call her friend. I'll go to the ends of earth if necessary. And I'll keep you both informed as to the progress we're making in finding this scumbag."

CHAPTER 17

I NEEDED TO put my mind at ease as I prepared to go to Northwestern Memorial Hospital's 40th Annual Celebration of Achievement Recognition Dinner, a prestigious event held downtown at the historic Palmer House Hilton Hotel on Monroe Street.

I passed several traffic lights, scanning the area, looking for a parking garage. It was much safer to park inside than on the street. After all, there were video cameras that could help deter a raging psychopath, weren't there?

I climbed out of my BMW, looking around, my heart now racing, not knowing whether I was being followed or watched. I quickly hurried around the corner, up the block and into the front entrance of the hotel.

As I walked in, a man quickly stepped in front of me, blocking my path. "Dr. Fields, how are you? I don't believe we've met. I'm Todd Coleman. I recently got started over in Gastroenterology, and I make it a point to introduce myself to those I work with."

"Hi, welcome aboard, and I hope I'm not terribly late?" I said as we walked toward the banquet room.

"No, you're fine. Most folks are just arriving. You'd think they would've had this on the weekend, or maybe a later time. C'mon, I'll escort you in."

"So, tell me, how do you like us so far?" I asked.

"I'm ecstatic. I've finally achieved my dream after years of busting my butt as an intern. But dealing with the long hours and the personal politics can make anyone insane after a while."

"I know exactly what you mean. I deal with it every day in the ER, and I have my own personal problems to contend with."

As we were being guided to our seats, a short man with a gray beard, glasses, and a large paunch pushing out the front of his slightly undersized two-piece suit walked to the podium at the front of the room, where he gently tapped on a live microphone.

"Hello, everyone, and welcome to this year's celebration of pioneers in the medical field. Tonight's presentation will recognize our distinguished recipients and honor their special achievements in the realm of medical excellence. So, without further ado, it is my pleasure to bring up the Administrator of Hospital Operations. Please give a warm welcome to Mr. Charles Okafor."

I applauded and watched Okafor as he made his way to the podium. I had heard good things about him, how he looked out for and supported staff whenever they were faced with disciplinary action, and how he stood up to lobbyists who sought to change how premiums were billed. But tonight my mind was elsewhere. I suddenly spotted Jasten Wier across the room and waved to get his attention.

I motioned him over to sit at our table. Perhaps his presence would divert Todd Coleman away from drooling over my cleavage.

Luckily, there was one seat left. Apparently, some doctor or staff person had decided not to attend.

Jasten was one of the first of my colleagues that I had warmed up to. He was really genuine, once you'd gotten past that satirical tone of his.

"Ah, familiar faces. Alexis, I've been looking for you. You're staying out of danger, I hope?" Jasten said as he took a seat.

"Well, you know me, Jasten. Staying out of danger for me is like a fish staying out of the water."

He chuckled.

Once all the guests were seated, the hotel staff quickly wheeled out dinner carts with plates consisting of prime rib of beef au jus, redskin mashed potatoes and balsamic-roasted vegetables.

As I watched numerous award presentations and some hired comedian's failed attempt at making anyone laugh during the entertainment segment, the evening went by pretty fast.

As the keynote speaker finished his closing remarks, Jasten and I stood up, grabbed our belongings, shook hands with whomever we'd recognized in the room, and walked outside of the hotel onto Monroe Street.

"So, what did you think about tonight?" he asked.

"I thought it was just okay. It's my first time attending. Although it's always good to show your face among the 'in' crowd. You know, do a little schmoozing?" I replied.

"Well, it *was* interesting. Nothing like sitting shoulder to shoulder with a bunch of stiff and stuck-up doctors," he said as we walked underneath the roar of the "L" train as it motored down the track. Then we took a sharp turn and headed to MB Allied Parking, where Jasten had parked his car.

"Usually I take what you say with a grain of salt, Jasten, but this time I'll have to agree with your non-politically correct observation."

Jasten chuckled. "Anybody who knows me well will tell you that I don't sugar-coat the truth, and I never—I mean not ever—rat on my friends," he offered in a fake Italian accent.

I laughed. "That's refreshing to hear. I need people in my life to show me exactly who they are, so I can believe them the first time!"

"Hey, honesty is my only policy, I say. And as promised, I'll see you to your car. Where'd you park?" he asked.

"I'm over at that ridiculously priced garage on the other side of Wabash Avenue. The one whose rates change as frequently as doctors in the ER."

"I'm glad you can joke about it. We'll get my car first. I'm right up the block, and I'll take you to yours. Speaking of which, I was able to get hold of what you wanted from my friend. Actually, I've got it in the car."

"You've got it already? You've got the gun?"

"Yep, and it's a sweet little lethal number. You'll see. I kept it locked in the glove compartment, because I didn't want my fiancée Brianna or my kids finding it in our place."

"Yeah, I completely understand, Jasten. Believe me, I understand."

Jasten and I walked into the vestibule of the garage where he had parked. "They've got these vending machine-style setups where you pay to get your car out," Justin said as he reached for the wallet in his back pocket. He pulled out his credit card and inserted it into the machine to pay. The receipt printed quickly. He grabbed it and wc took the elevator up to the second level, where I followed him to his SUV, a dark brown Buick Enclave he'd purchased for his budding family.

"I'm over here, not too far." Jasten pulled out his car key fob and unlocked the doors. He looked around before opening the passenger side door, inserted his key into the glove box, and gripped the gun he'd obtained for me. It was neatly packaged in a black carrying case. "This is it," he said, lifting the chunky black pistol out and handing it over.

"Yeah, this should do," I said as I felt its weight in my hand. "You did ask your friend if it's clean?"

"Absolutely. I made sure of it. I trust him. We go a long way back," he said.

"How much do I owe you for it?"

"His price is three hundred. Non-negotiable and all cash. I tried to see if he'd go lower, but he said he couldn't, especially after going through the trouble of finding exactly what you wanted."

"Okay, I'll have the cash for you tomorrow. You trust me?" I said, and smiled.

"Of course. You take it home with you tonight, familiarize yourself with it and pay me tomorrow."

"Deal."

"Is this thing loaded? Ready to go?" I asked.

"Yeah, but be careful. He said it's got a full clip, including one round in the chamber. I told you, this guy knows his stuff and he doesn't mess around. You ever use one before?"

"I have, but it wasn't exactly what I'd call a run-of-the-mill situation. It was when that cop attacked me in Lake Park."

"You shot a cop?"

"Yeah. He raped me, and then tried to kill my friend and me because we were going to testify against him and his partners in crime. They were some diabolically crooked scumbags."

"Well, I'm glad you got away. And if I were you, I'd only have that thing out if I'm going to use it."

I tucked the gun in my purse and then watched Jasten as he walked toward the rear of the vehicle and leaned over.

"There's some type of hissing sound. Do you hear that?" he asked.

I knelt closer to the wheel, trying to figure out where the hissing sound was coming from.

Suddenly a dark-colored Impala careened around the corner at a high rate of speed. The driver, it seemed, was gunning it directly toward Jasten and me as we stood behind the vehicle talking.

We flew out of the way as the missile on wheels came at us. We both tumbled to the ground as the speeding car crashed into the rear bumper of Jasten's Enclave. The driver, who had donned a Black Hawks cap, smirked as he yanked the gear shift into reverse, backed the car up, then sat momentarily, staring out the front windshield, clearly wondering if he had managed to hit Jasten or me.

"Somebody's trying to kill us!" Jasten yelled.

"I'm over here, Jasten," I called out from between a pair of parked vehicles.

The thug was still out there, waiting to run us over. Then, almost as if on cue, Jasten and I darted out from the parked cars we'd been hiding between and ran for our lives through the parking garage. The madman in the Impala shifted back into gear and the car screeched toward us in a rubbery cloud of smoke.

Jasten and I bolted, then turned a corner, frantically opened the nearest door and ran down a stairwell as the Impala made an abrupt U-turn, swerved around to ground level and screamed out of the garage, crashing through the exit's ticket gate.

I stood panting at the bottom of the stairwell, wondering what had just happened. "What the hell was that all about?" I managed in between breaths.

"I'll tell you what—the next time we meet, it'll be in front of a police station. You are just too fucking dangerous to hang out with!" Jasten shot back.

"I'm sorry I got you into this. You should probably stay away from me until I can get all this resolved."

We hobbled up the concrete steps of the stairwell. When we reached the level where Jasten's Enclave was parked, we stuck our heads out to see if the coast was clear. Whoever the son of a bitch in the Impala had been, he was gone now. We nervously walked through the garage.

"You going to call the police?" Jasten asked.

"I will, but there's not much I could tell them they don't already know. They know someone's after me and they have a good idea who it is. It's just a matter of catching up with him."

Jasten and I cautiously approached his SUV.

"Jasten, I'm so sorry about your car," I said as we surveyed the damage to the rear bumper and quarter panel.

"Hey, don't sweat it. I'll just file a claim and get it fixed. In the meantime, let's get the hell out of here."

"I'm hoping you can still drive it. I'm praying it'll start."

"We'll see. Let's not hang around here any longer. I can take you to your car now," he said.

Jasten had barely finished talking when a small group of men in dark suits and sunglasses exited the elevator and began walking toward us.

"Get in!"

Jasten shoved the key into the ignition and backed out of the parking space. He circled around several rows of vehicles and concrete pillars before we found ourselves on street level.

"Who the hell were they?" I muttered.

"I have no idea, and we weren't sticking around to find out."

Jasten merged into traffic and drove me to the garage where I had parked my BMW.

"Hurry. I'll stay out here with my hazards on until I see you come out safely. And I hope you find the son of a bitch who's after you," he said.

Before I climbed out of Jasten's car, I opened my purse and lifted the gun out its case, then peered at him intently. "You know this bullet, the one you told me that's in the chamber?" I said.

"Yeah, what about it?"

"It's got his name on it," I said.

I gave Jasten a thank you nod and got out of the car, then spun around to enter the building. After paying the parking fee, I hurried up to level 4, climbed in my X5, then drove around to street level, inserted my ticket in the automated attendant and gave Jasten a wave before peeling away.

CHAPTER **18**

APPROXIMATELY NINE MILES to the north in East Rogers Park, a tall, wiry man wearing a disturbing speech-equipped mask waited for Jasten Wier to exit the two-story colonial home he shared with his fiancée and children. It had been raining all morning.

After kissing his fiancée, Brianna, goodbye, Wier came jogging down the wooden steps of his porch at exactly 6:30 a.m. Timed to the minute. Like clockwork.

The would-be killer had sat in his stakeout position for three days in a row, patiently waiting for this moment.

After Wier got into his car, fitted the key in the ignition and maneuvered his vehicle to pull out, the masked man put his car in drive, sped forward and blocked Wier from leaving his parking space.

Wier craned his head and blew his horn in frustration.

"C'mon. I'm trying to get out!" he yelled, waving his hands, baffled.

The man didn't move. Didn't flinch. He just stared through slightly tinted windows as raindrops pelted each of their vehicles.

Wier peered out his driver's side window and blew his horn again. Slowly, his agitation grew to a dangerous level. His fiancée had heard the blare of the horn, and he saw her push the curtains aside to look out the window. He had had enough. He got out of his Buick Enclave and looped around to confront the other driver. He crouched over.

"Will you move your friggin' car, asshole? I'm trying to get to work!"

The man looked at Wier, then electronically lowered his side window. Wier's eyes widened with shock when he saw the hideous-looking black polycarbonate mask staring back at him.

What the fuck? Who the hell is this dickwad? he thought.

Suddenly, a weird, metallic, electronic-sounding voice spat back. "Sir, I'm hearing impaired. Can you please come closer and repeat what you just said?"

Wier crouched over again, his eyes meeting the man's. "I said I'm late for work, and I need you to move your fucking car!"

The man sat there unfazed, his car's motor still running.

Wier yelled again. "What? Are you deaf and dumb too? Or are you just plain fucking crazy?"

The man finally had something else to say.

"It would be the latter," he replied as he calmly lifted up a Glock nine millimeter and shot Wier point-blank in the head.

Blood sprayed out of the back of Wier's head. He tried to speak, but only a gurgling sound escaped his throat. His body quickly went slack as he crashed backwards onto the wet asphalt.

The killer then punched the gas and sped down the block before making a squealing left turn.

Wier's fiancée, a nurse, had watched in horror as it all happened. She was screaming as she ran outside in the pouring rain.

"Oh, God, no!"

She knelt down and cradled Weir's head on top of her left arm as she frantically dialed 911 with her right hand. "I want to report a shooting," she cried out to the emergency dispatcher.

"My fiancé's just been murdered."

CHAPTER 19

I STAYED HOME for several days after getting the call about Jasten's murder. It was completely and utterly devastating. I was afraid to leave my condo, even to go to work.

There's an adage that fear stands for False Evidence Appearing Real. Well, my fear was as real as it got. Feeling distraught, I contemplated leaving Chicago, leaving the position I had worked so hard to obtain.

But I had invested too much in getting here, so quitting was never really an option. I struggled to remain strong in the midst of immense tragedy.

I walked across the room and grabbed my purse, then thumbed through all of the contacts in my new cell phone, ready to call every police officer, detective and FBI agent I could think of. *Hey, guys, I need a little help here!*

I hoped they would give Jasten's murder investigation all the attention it so rightly deserved.

The only person I was able to reach was FBI Special Agent Preston Ponder, who agreed to meet to go over the latest developments in the investigation.

In a few days Jasten would be laid to rest, and attending his funeral would be one of the saddest things I'd had to endure since leaving Lake Park. Almost as sad as the time when I was a kid and my mother had told me curtly, "Daddy isn't coming home anymore."

In the short time I had known Jasten, he had made such a favorable impression on me and most of the staff who knew him that I wondered who could have wanted to kill him.

Could it have been the same person who'd almost killed us in what had seemed a targeted attack that night in the parking garage?

As I sat at my kitchen table thinking about the camaraderie and fun times that Jasten and I had shared, I broke out into uncontrollable sobs. Tears poured from my eyes like water flowing from a tap.

Suddenly, there was a crisp knock at my door.

"Who is it?" I managed, wiping my now bloodshot eyes with the backs of my hands.

"Are you okay, Ms. Alex?" came a recognizable voice from out in the hall.

I smiled. It was Terrell Burton, my buddy, the nice kid who lived several units down. I opened the door. He was standing there wearing a look of deep concern.

"Come in, Terrell. How are you?"

"I'm good. But I knocked on your door because it sounded like you were crying. You okay?" he asked again.

"I could be better," I replied. "I just found out that a good friend of mine was killed. He and I worked together."

Terrell's eyes widened. I could tell, for a moment, that he was at a loss for words.

"Oh, wow. I'm sorry to hear that. How'd he die?"

"He apparently got into an argument with someone in front of his house and they shot him to death."

"That's awful," Terrell said.

"Yeah, I know. And I hate to be the bearer of such sad news this morning, Terrell. But if there's one kernel of wisdom you can take from something like this, it's simply to cherish life and the people around you. We never know what each day will bring, and tomorrow's not promised to any of us."

"Okay. I will," he said.

"Thank you. And thanks for listening to me this morning," I said, and smiled. "There's one other thing. It may not be best for you to hang around me right now. I think someone's trying to hurt me, and I don't want you getting hurt in the process."

"Why would someone want to hurt you, Ms. Alex? You're a nice person. I don't understand."

"Well, there are some evil and sick people out there in the world, and we have to be careful with everything we do. We have to make better decisions. That'll hopefully keep us safe."

"If anyone tries to hurt you, Ms. Alex, just remember, I've got your back," Terrell snapped boldly.

"Well, that's very noble of you, Terrell. I could use a guardian angel right about now."

Yes, indeed.

CHAPTER **20**

FBI SPECIAL AGENT Preston Ponder was on his way to see me, to discuss what he called "a few tactical issues" we'd need to implement before the weekend.

I was all in for whatever the FBI and the Chicago PD had planned, determined to put an end to this nightmare once and for all.

At 7:35 he sent me a text saying that he was outside and on his way up to my condo.

I stepped to the window to confirm that it was actually him and watched as he climbed out of a gleaming black SUV, adjusted his shirt and tie, and walked into the building.

I buzzed him in and immediately breathed a sigh of relief, for as long as he was here this evening, I would feel at ease.

A minute or two later I heard the elevator chime, then heard footsteps heading toward my door. I could always hear when someone was pacing these shoddily constructed hallways. And for me, that was a good thing.

I opened the door and he stood before me holding a leather briefcase in his right hand. He was wearing a pin-striped black suit, crisp white shirt, black tie, and had what looked like Wayfarers covering his eyes.

"Agent Ponder," I greeted him, welcoming him in.

"Dr. Fields. It's a pleasure to meet again."

He angled toward the living room, surveying my condo. I wondered what he was thinking.

"Pretty chic and cozy place you've got here. This area has changed drastically over the years. A lot of new construction," he said, glancing out the window at the high-rise coming up across the street.

I was amazed by his familiarity with the area. "I was under the impression that you're stationed in Chicago temporarily," I said.

He turned to look at me. "I pretty much travel wherever I'm needed. I'm not one to brag, but to be honest, I've been appointed to lead a special, newly formed Violent Crime Apprehension Unit, targeting what the Bureau would consider its most violent, highest-profile cases."

"Well, I guess congratulations are in order. You're obviously very accomplished. Can I offer you anything? Bottled water? Juice?"

"No, but thank you. About twenty minutes ago I finished some deep dish pizza and a spinach salad. Some of Chicago's finest and I had lunch together over on Wabash Avenue." Ponder chuckled. "It was supposed to be some leisurely bonding among comrades, but all we talked about was work—which leads me to you. I'd like to talk to you about a strategy I've put together to try to solve this case and, hopefully, the recent murders that have occurred nearby."

"Okay. I'm all ears."

"May I?" He was asking if he could set his briefcase on top of my glass cocktail table, using it as a makeshift desk to discuss his idea.

I nodded. He set the black attaché down and flipped open the clasps on each side, then raised the top half. He pulled out several stacks of papers, including a much larger sheet that had been folded in half.

"I've got the details of the plan I'd like to implement. Because experience tells me that this scumbag is planning his next attack."

He laid out what looked like the entire map of Chicago. There were clusters of symbols inside larger geographical patterns. I looked in astonishment at the intricate markings and the meticulous handiwork.

"This is very impressive," I said. "Though I'm not sure exactly what I'm looking at."

"Don't worry. Let me explain." He pointed. "This area here represents Chicago's central region, and neighborhoods where the most violent crimes have occurred. The two highlighted areas mark the locations where the bodies of Hagenstock and Collier were found. This red area here marks your location, where the suspect's IP address was traced to. Whoever communicated with Taylor Hagenstock the night she was murdered did so from this building," he explained.

"Yes," I said. "That's what I've been told."

"So, there's a connection based on the evidence we've gathered. Unless someone just randomly selected your name as a decoy to throw law enforcement off track, which isn't very likely, by the way, then someone is purposely trying to implicate you in her murder."

I shook my head. "I should have followed my gut and called you sooner. My coworker Jasten and I were attacked the other night after leaving the Palmer House Hilton. We'd been there for an industry event, and were headed to our vehicles, which were parked in a public garage, when someone tried to run us over. Several days later, Jasten was murdered in front of his house—in what was classified a road rage incident. Though I can't understand why anyone would want to kill him."

"Is there any description of the attacker? License plate? Did you notify the police?"

"No, I didn't. There's been so much happening lately, constantly, every day. But after that incident, and finding that newspaper article, I knew it was time to go a different route, and I wanted to speak to you personally."

Ponder shrugged. "Often, there's no rhyme or reason when we're dealing with these psychopaths and scumbags. There's usually an underlying cause that would never make sense to the rest of us." He continued, "I know what you've gone through, what you went through in Lake Park. And I really want to help you, Dr. Fields. But the Bureau will need your complete cooperation on every level. Your involvement could mean a greater chance of solving this case, and of course, saving your life."

"Okay. I'm all for it. What do you need from me?"

"Well, for starters, I'd like for you to continue living in your condo, going about your day-to-day activities, as if nothing is out of the ordinary. With the cooperation of the Chicago police, we'll set up a surveillance operation, watching you as you go to and from your condo to the hospital, or wherever else your day should take you. Of course, you'll have to say goodbye to some of your privacy. We'll also need an itinerary of where you're going, who you're meeting with, and a list of family, friends, and work staff that you have contact with on a frequent basis." Ponder reached into his suit pocket, pulled out a small jewelry case and flipped it open. "I'd like to give you this watch to wear."

"Why? What does it do?"

"It's fitted with a miniature GPS tracking device that will allow us to monitor your whereabouts in the unfortunate event you go missing. It's certainly not the prettiest of timepieces, but it gets the job done."

I took off the stainless steel Movado that I'd been wearing and replaced it with the unassuming watch he'd given me.

"Lastly, I suggest that we install surveillance cameras strategically throughout your condo. It's imperative that we see who has access to your unit when you're not home. And one other important thing. You may be asked to wear a wire—to help incriminate the suspect if you have the opportunity to engage him in conversation."

My eyes bored into his. I swallowed hard. "Am I at risk doing this?"

"There *is* some degree of risk, unfortunately, and your level of involvement is completely at your discretion, of course. I can assure you that we'll be watching your every move, and we'll be ready to apprehend anyone who's looking to harm you, in any way."

I took a deep breath, thinking about putting my life at risk. But my life was already at risk, wasn't it? At least now, I could have the Chicago police and the FBI watching my back.

"Okay. I'll do it," I said. "Anything to bring an end to this madness."

Ponder continued, "I know it's asking a lot of your time, and you're a doctor, which means you're incredibly busy. But I appreciate your willingness to embark on what would be a terrifying ordeal for most people. I think you're doing the right thing. You won't notice many changes, aside from the inconveniences."

He neatly folded the statistical map he'd brought with him, laid it in his briefcase and snapped the clasps shut. "We can get started right away. Time is of the essence here, and we have no idea what he's capable of doing next, be it Bachman or someone else."

"I haven't seen or talked to him since the night he assaulted me," I said. "I can only imagine his increased rage and instability ever since his mother was shot and killed by the police in Madison. He's lost everything that ever meant anything to him, and now, I believe—in his mind—there's no turning back"

CHAPTER 21

BEUREGARD CALLED Taylor Hagenstock's friend Michelle Darcy for an interview, which was scheduled for later that evening at 6 p.m. Once the brief and informative meeting with Travis and Donna Hagenstock had concluded, the detective jumped in his car and headed for the expressway to return to headquarters.

After leaving work on the north side, Darcy drove to the 1st District police headquarters downtown for her meeting with Beuregard. She parked her car, entered the building, and after several tense minutes, was escorted upstairs to Homicide.

She was wearing a gray overcoat, a pink cardigan and black slacks. She was young and pretty, and her hair was pulled back into a ponytail.

Beuregard stood up and walked around his desk, motioning for her to come inside his office.

"Ms. Darcy, thank you for coming down on such short notice," he said as he extended his hand.

"Hi. Pleased to meet you," she responded.

Beuregard gestured for her to sit down, then returned to his chair. "As I said earlier, I want to find out more about your friend Taylor, and anything that could possibly help us turn the corner in the investigation. I'm sure you can appreciate that."

"I can. That was my girl. We grew up together. We were more like sisters than friends. And I still think about her every day."

"It's tough, I know. So, I'll get right to it if you don't mind." Beuregard reared back in his chair and clenched his hands on top of his head. "Ms. Darcy, I read Taylor's blog and found out that she was actually pregnant at the time of her death. Were you aware of that?"

Darcy turned her gaze away from Beuregard. Her pulse hammered. She swallowed hard. "No, I wasn't aware of that," she said.

Beuregard paused momentarily, sizing the young woman up as his eyes met hers. "I'll tell you what I think. I think you might've been. And I'd appreciate it if you were honest with me. Actually, whatever you're hiding could hurt this case more than anything."

Darcy dropped her head as she remained silent.

"Everything you say can stay confidential between you and me, if that makes you feel any better," said Beuregard.

Darcy took a deep breath and shook her head. "Um, okay, I'm a bit nervous here. But, no, there's nothing else I can think of, really. Taylor was a very private person and we weren't in contact as much as we were when we attended school together."

Beuregard straightened up, leaning forward across his desk, glaring straight on at Darcy. "You know, something tells me you're holding back more than what you're letting on, Ms. Darcy. And quite frankly, my patience is wearing thin." Beuregard raised his voice. "Now, it would be in your best interest to share whatever additional information you have that could help with our investigation, or suffer the damn consequences!"

Darcy blew out a nervous breath. "Okay. Okay. I promised I would never share her secret… but Taylor also worked as an escort in addition to her regular gig. She desperately wanted out of her parents' house, but she wasn't quite making enough to live how she wanted. So she joined some shady North Side agency. They promised to screen their clients and keep her real identity a secret. She went by the nickname Girl Friday."

"Oh? How original," Beuregard said sarcastically.

"I know, right? But Taylor thought it was cute and funny. She put ads on various websites, including some of the erotic chatrooms, advertising her services. That's probably how she met up with the scumbag who killed her."

"Who'd she get pregnant by?"

"Okay, that's a whole other story. One day Taylor and I were at this bar on Rush Street. We were both stressed from work and met up for Happy Hour. We'd been dancing and getting drunk, and suddenly, out of the blue, Taylor sees Adam Talbert. He's a guy we went to college with and her first and only boyfriend before she started dating women. They talked, catching up on the latest. He was all over her. Later, she told me that when we left the bar, she went back to his place, and he pretty much took advantage of her.

She paused for a moment, then went on, "She didn't report it, figuring that no one would believe her. Anyway, she found out she was pregnant, and was trying to decide if she wanted to keep the baby when she was murdered. It really weighed heavily on her mind, because she knew deep down that her parents had always looked forward to having a grandchild."

"Is that everything?" Beuregard asked.

"I swear. That's everything I know."

"Okay. So, take some solace in knowing that what you've disclosed here today can be helpful in some way. I'm sure Taylor would be appreciative of it."

Darcy took another deep breath. "I hope so. It was definitely the right thing to do."

"Thank you for coming down this evening, Ms. Darcy. I'll be in touch."

"Please do. I want to do my part to help solve this case. Like you said, Taylor's counting on it."

Darcy stood up, shook Beuregard's hand, buttoned her overcoat and walked outside the homicide unit to go home.

The detective pulled out a notepad and pen to jot down some notes from the conversation. Suddenly, Kirkendall strolled into the office and shut the door.

"These just came in. Take a look," he said as he tossed a stack of paper-clipped documents onto the large metal desk.

Beuregard flipped through Hagenstock's autopsy report, glancing at the toxicology section. "Cause and manner of death, homicide. No surprise there. But here's the smoking gun," he said as he scrolled down further, swallowed hard, and looked up at Kirkendall. "It's confirmed. She was pregnant."

"So we're looking at a double murder now, without question," Kirkendall said.

"Her friend claimed that Hagenstock hooked up with an old boyfriend, went back to his place, apparently had sex with the guy, and allegedly got pregnant by him. His name's Adam Talbert."

"That'll be easy to confirm. He's a person of interest, and we need to find him. Think her friend is telling us everything she knows?"

"I believe so. I had to press her to get her to open up. I'll stay in touch with her."

Kirkendall nodded and put his hands in the pockets of his navy gabardine pants before turning to leave. "You do that. She just might prove to be a key player before this is over."

CHAPTER **22**

THE FBI FOLLOWED through on their promise to beef up my security in an effort to keep me safe. They installed several small surveillance cameras in my condominium unit, through which they could monitor any unauthorized entry.

This whole thing was utterly weird to me. I felt like Jim Carrey's character in the movie *The Truman Show*. There was a certain protocol I had to follow each and every time I ventured out.

Undoubtedly, the FBI wouldn't typically go to such extremes with an individual like yours truly. But because my case involved a larger-than-life crime plot, or, depending on how you looked at it, one integral piece of a serial killer's sick and twisted game, Agent Ponder had the go-ahead to implement his plan however he saw fit.

Lucky me. I was practically trapped inside my home, leaving only to run to the store and go to work.

I felt a little more at ease now that the Feds were watching my back, but I also wondered if anyone took the liberty of watching when I was at home. The deal was for them to monitor my condo, but only in the event I was away.

I could no longer stand being inside and ached to do a disappearing act. I had taken some time off work, several days to be exact, and wanted to cheer myself up by going shopping.

I sent a text to a number I'd been given to alert the Bureau as to what time I would be leaving and where I would be going. I threw on my coat, grabbed my cell phone and left at roughly 7 p.m. All I could think about was a lovely pair of Jimmy Choos I had seen online, and had been wanting forever.

Neiman Marcus on Michigan Avenue was having a huge sale. I couldn't get there fast enough. When I finally arrived at the store, the pumps looked even more fabulous than they had in cyberspace.

After I'd snagged the last pair in my size, it suddenly dawned on me that there were some important files stored on a flash drive that I'd left in my office. I needed to complete the files before I returned from my short leave of absence, and stopped by the hospital for the near-capacity memory stick.

The night shift consisted mostly of a skeleton crew. General Operations was a lot more tranquil, sans the occasional gunshot, stabbing, or accident victim coming into the ER.

As I walked down the hall, I saw several nurses who knew both me and Jasten.

"Alexis, how're you holding up?" one asked, concerned.

"As well as can be expected," I replied. "Taking a little time off, one day at a time before I come back."

"Jasten was so nice. We're going to miss him!" one of the RNs blurted. "You take care. Let us know if you need anything."

"Thanks, ladies."

I continued down the corridor toward the employee parking lot, and noticed that what looked like another doctor in blue scrubs and a surgical mask was walking hurriedly behind me.

I padded up to the bank of elevators in the center of the hall and pushed the lighted down button to go to the underground level.

"Can you hold it for me?" came a voice from behind me. It was the other doctor, catching up to go down as well. "You're Dr. Fields?" he asked as he joined me inside the elevator.

"Yes," I said.

"I've heard about you," he said congenially through the mask.

I glanced at him, wondering why he still had the mask on outside of a surgical environment. He must have noticed my frown, because he quickly removed it.

"Oh, I'm sorry. I didn't mean to be rude. I'm Dr. Sitnikov," he said with what sounded like a heavy Russian accent. "I'm new to Chicago. I work in the Oncology Center."

"I'm in the ER," I told him. "At least for now."

The elevator reached the garage level and we both walked out. His car was parked about twenty feet away, and I watched him as he tapped the button on his key fob, opened the rear door, reached into the back seat and pulled out a black parka.

I had conveniently parked further down in the same aisle. "Goodnight, nice meeting you," I said.

"Likewise," he replied.

I turned and walked several steps, then, suddenly, I heard the sound of running feet. Before I could swivel around, a hand had forcefully gripped my mouth, covering part of my nostrils as well, and a large handgun was firmly planted against my right temple.

"Walk, and don't say a fucking word," the Russian-accented voice whispered in my ear. "You scream and I'll shoot you right here."

I grunted and could barely breathe as my eyes welled with tears. *Dear God, what is going on? Where is he taking me?*

We stayed tethered together as we walked to his car. He opened the trunk with his keyless remote before pushing me backwards.

"Please don't do this," I said. "The FBI is watching me. You won't get away with this!"

"I've been sent to torture you, and then kill you. And that's all that matters," he snapped, then he shoved me into the trunk.

My legs were dangling over the top of the rear bumper. He tucked his gun away, then he slammed the trunk down on top of my legs.

"A little token, to make sure you don't run," he muttered.

The pain was excruciating. A part of me felt like I'd died right there in that parking lot. I started to waver in and out of consciousness. He stuffed a handkerchief in my mouth and tied my hands and feet with an orange extension cord. Then he pushed my legs inside the trunk and shut it again, leaving me to whimper in this pitch-black, confined torture chamber.

I could hear the engine start, then the car went screeching backwards to pull out of the space as I tumbled about.

He drove out of the parking lot, the car bouncing up and down as he exited onto East Huron Street. My cell phone had been tucked away in my purse. But the son of a bitch had been smart enough to take my purse from me and toss it in the back seat.

This is it. I'm going to die tonight, I thought. *Gee, that's really smart of you Alexis, to go somewhere other than Neiman Marcus, and not inform the FBI where you detoured to.*

About twenty soul-annihilating minutes later, the car took several turns, then rolled onto what sounded like gravel and stopped. The scumbag seemed to have reached his destination. I could hear him kill the engine, get out, and walk toward the back of the car.

I then heard several beeps in rapid succession. The trunk popped open. I squinted into the darkness, at the lights in the distance, at his large silhouette in front of the moon's amber glow. Whoever this guy was, he was powerfully built.

He scooped me up like I was a sack of flour and draped me over his shoulder. I moaned and whimpered, scanning the area as he carried me toward an old, apparently abandoned building. A warehouse, I thought.

He pried open a metal door, then carried me inside to a cold, dark room, and threw me onto a hard wooden chair. I snorted back a wet sob.

This place, wherever he had taken me, didn't have any heat. I shivered as I watched him walk to a nearby table, flip open some type of steel toolbox, and pull out what looked like a large carving knife.

Please, God, no. What's he going to do with that?

He pulled up a chair and sat in front of me, glaring.

"Before I torture and kill you, I'm going to tell you exactly why I'm doing it. I was instructed to tell you the reason," he offered coldly. "You pissed off a lot of important people in Lake Park. Powerful people. The kind you don't want to fuck with. And because of you, the Feds took down El Subida, a million dollar a month operation," he went on. "You should have just stayed in your place like a good neighbor and kept your mouth shut. It was I who came to visit you several times in your condo. I left the newspaper article for you in your bathroom. Just a reminder of what a naughty little bitch you are, eh? Now, your punishment will be for me to remove your tongue and send it to the people I work for as a souvenir. And *then,* I kill you!"

He stood and moved close to me. My heart was beating madly as he snatched the crumpled handkerchief from my mouth.

He violently grabbed my face, squeezing strongly with his left hand. "Stick your tongue out," he said, his eyes boring into mine.

Suddenly, I heard the sound of a fleet of vehicles pulling up outside. He let go of me, his gaze pinballing around the room. Clearly, he had no idea who was approaching.

A moment later, a swarm of FBI agents and Chicago police officers burst through the door.

"Drop that knife and back away from her!" one of the agents barked.

I recognized the voice. It was Preston Ponder. I closed my eyes and took a deep breath. "Thank you, God!" I muttered as the cops rushed forward and took the Russian into custody.

"You okay?" Ponder asked.

"Except for my legs," I answered. "He smashed them with the trunk lid."

"Somebody help me here!" Ponder barked, and then knelt down. "Let's get this cord off her and help her stand. She's been injured."

He and another agent untied the electrical cord I'd been bound with and lifted me up, bookending me as I hobbled out to a waiting SUV.

"Make sure to get her an ambulance," one of the agents called out.

"I don't need an ambulance. I can go to the hospital on my own. Those guys already have enough on their plate," I said. "Just drop me off at the ER." *Once again, I'm a patient, a victim, instead of being the one doing the treating,* I thought.

Then I remembered something. "My purse. It's in that car," I blurted to one of the cops, pointing at the vehicle I'd been transported in.

One of the agents opened the door, grabbed my purse and gave it to me. They assisted me in climbing inside the SUV. My legs were still acutely painful, with bleeding lacerations, possibly fractured. I wouldn't know for sure until I could get them properly evaluated.

"How did you guys find me?" I asked with childlike curiosity.

"The watch," Ponder responded. "The high-tech timepiece I gave you allowed us to track your location in the event we failed to hear from you. We received your text that you were headed to Neiman Marcus, which closed about an hour ago. When we texted and called without getting a response, we knew something was wrong. And obviously, we arrived here just in time."

I sat next to Ponder in the back of the vehicle, and two other agents occupied the front. These guys totally looked the part: clean shaven, dressed in suits, earwigs in their ears, with a serious take no shit demeanor, almost like Secret Service agents protecting the president.

"I wonder if it's finally over," I said aloud as we pulled away.

"These cases are like putting together pieces of a puzzle," Ponder said. "So far we've got one piece in place. And the guy we apprehended tonight may have been the one trying to kill you initially. What would have been his motive?"

"He was a hired hit man sent to kill me for my part in El Subida's downfall. He said that himself," I responded.

Ponder nodded and said, "If they've tried once and failed, another attempt could be forthcoming. I'm not trying to alarm you right now, but when the indictments were issued, the main focus was on the key players, whoever we were confident we could successfully prosecute. That still leaves the possibility of some lone wolf, hell-bent on payback."

CHAPTER **23**

I SPENT THE next several days in the hospital and resting in my condo. Special Agent Ponder assisted me along the way, helping me get home in the wheelchair I'd been given to use until my fractured shins were healed.

While at home, feeling sorry for myself, I got an unexpected call from him.

"Hi, there. You called to check up on me?" I said, and chuckled.

"That, and to give you the latest, which I hope you'll find comforting," he said.

I was ready for any type of good news that could stop this train wreck of a life I'd been living.

"What's the latest?" I asked curiously.

"Well, we raked over that Russian scumbag pretty rigorously during interrogation, and he gave up some new players that we've got in custody now. They're awaiting trial, no bond, and the state's case against them looks promising. I'll keep you abreast as this unfolds."

"Thank you."

"How are you holding up?" he asked.

"My legs are still sore, although the painkillers I'm taking have helped. It's tough getting around in a wheelchair when you're used to being upright and walking wherever you want."

"I can't begin to imagine what you're feeling. But looking at it from a positive angle, it could have been a lot worse. That being said, have you received any other threats? Experienced anything else suspicious in nature?"

"Not at all. And I'm thankful."

"We're still with you every step of the way. Be diligent, stay safe, and consider having someone stay with you until you get back on your feet. No pun intended. And don't hesitate to call."

"Got it," I replied.

I hung up the phone and wheeled myself into the kitchen to check out the fridge for a light meal. I didn't have much of an appetite, but I needed to eat.

Let's see, smoked turkey club on Ciabatta, apple and walnut salad, assorted chilled fruit. There's nothing warm in here?

Suddenly my phone rang. I did an about-face into my living room to find the phone buried under a stack of papers and folders that had toppled over on my cocktail table.

I glanced at the caller ID and pressed the speaker button to talk hands free. "Mom, how goes it?" I said.

"I should be asking you that question," she replied.

Right then, I knew that my mother might have some telepathic sense of what was going on in my life, or perhaps it was her motherly intuition.

I hadn't told her that I'd been assaulted again, or that Wilfred had supposedly been seen in Chicago. She'd been through enough, including being recently diagnosed with arterial hypertension, so getting her riled up was the last thing I wanted.

"I've got Carol on the line three-way. We're calling to tell you we plan on coming up to Chicago to visit. I'll be on vacation and Carol said she can get time off. So plan on it, Ms. I Want to Be Independent. By the way, how are your legs?" my mom asked.

"My legs?" I answered coyly.

"Someone mentioned on Facebook that you'd had some sort of leg injury."

"I did, but I'm doing better now, Mom. I've taken some time off work—a much-needed break from the madness of the emergency room."

"I understand. But don't be a stranger. You could call more often, you know. I find out more about what's going on in your life from Facebook than I do talking to you."

"I apologize. I promise to keep in touch and tell you everything that unfolds in my crazy, never-a-dull-moment life. Good or bad!"

"Excellent. Well, I'm going to let Carol take over. I've got to get to my Zumba class. They're keen on us being on time."

"Okay, mother dear. Have fun, and don't overwork yourself."

Carol chimed in. "Hi, girlfriend. Sorry to hear about your leg injury."

"Thanks, Carol. I didn't want my mother to worry, but I've been through yet another rough patch."

"Like what?"

"I was violently attacked by some hired creep sent here by El Subida, that rogue criminal cop ring I helped expose in Lake Park. They frigging put a hit out on me! They obviously must still have a presence up there. Though, after the police and FBI rescued me, they had this guy give up the names of the people who sent him. The evil son of a bitch slammed a trunk lid on my legs, and that's the real, fucked-up reason I'm in a wheelchair."

"That's crazy! I'm so glad you're okay otherwise. Your life is starting to sound like some damned murder mystery novel. And Wilfred? Any word about him?"

"He's been seen in the area. Of course, I heard the same thing when I was in Lake Park, but I never had any contact with him. Which is fine by me."

"After the police shot and killed his mother, I can only imagine what must be going through that moronic skull of his. And if he ever found out that the real reason you lost interest was because you started up with that handsome med student, he would have gone ballistic."

I said, "That guy was the greatest. But we couldn't stay together—he got an offer from some pediatric hospital in Seattle. And a long-distance relationship was just not what I'd envisioned. But he was such an improvement over Wilfred, emotionally, sexually, and he treated me like I was the only woman who mattered in the world."

"Sounds like a great catch that got away. Do you still have the restraining order against Wilfred?"

"Yeah, and I'll keep it as long as I feel threatened. Speaking of which, I've got a gun now. A cute little semiautomatic."

Carol roared back in sweet surprise. "Well, it's about time. Good for you. It may come in handy. And learn how to use it. What made you reconsider?"

"My safety, of course. I got it from my coworker Jasten, a wonderful guy, who apparently was killed in some sort of road rage incident."

"I'm sorry to hear that."

"What makes it so bad is that his fiancée witnessed the shooting. Right in front of their house. Shot point blank in the head. He'd recently gotten engaged, and he had two kids."

"Shit, that's awful. I guess Chicago is holding true to its infamous reputation of being a crime-ridden hell hole."

"Well, like most cities, some areas are better than others, but crime is everywhere. Of course, I see the effects of it every day. You have to prepare for it mentally, although you can never really get used to it. A few days ago, we tried to save a baby who'd been rushed in after being shot in the head. After the emotional trauma of that night, I was completely and utterly zonked."

"That's awful. And then you have your own personal issues to deal with. I still can't get over hearing that Wilfred's mother was accused of beating your neighbor to death."

"According to the police in Madison, she admitted to murdering him before she herself was shot and killed that day. And she admitted to killing her husband too."

"That whole damned family seemed bat-shit crazy and one hundred percent dysfunctional, if you ask me," Carol said.

"Actually, just the mention of his name wrangles my nerves, which are already frazzled. That said, I seriously need to find something to eat, girlfriend."

"Okay, well, eat some for both of us. I'm stuck here at work and won't be free for another two hours. And take care of yourself, Alexis."

"I will. Oh, and keep me in your prayers. Bye."

After talking to Carol I warmed up some vegetarian chili I'd found in the fridge before turning on the TV and digging into a tasty bowl of salted caramel gelato, one of my serious, hard habit to break guilty pleasures.

I grabbed the remote and flipped through various channels, looking for anything that could transport my mind elsewhere, away from my current hellish existence.

I was startled by a brisk knock on the door. I set down the remote, then wheeled myself around and headed for the door. Of course, I couldn't stand up to look out of the peephole.

"Who is it?" I called out.

"It's me, Terrell, Ms. Alex," came the quick response from the hall.

I opened the door and saw Terrell standing there looking visibly shaken, nervously stammering, trying to speak.

"I... I... um..."

Suddenly, almost magically, materializing behind him was a hideous-looking woman. She raised a shiny, glimmering knife. "I think what he's trying to tell you is that he's got a knife to his throat."

It was Wilfred. I'd recognize that voice anywhere.

"Get your ass inside. Move it!" he ordered.

I backed up my wheelchair as Wilfred shoved Terrell inside, still holding that knife to his throat while armlocking his neck. It looked like the same dagger he'd held to my throat in Madison.

"Wilfred, please, he has nothing to do with this. Whatever you want from me, fine. But please, just let him go!" I pleaded.

Shaking his head, Wilfred marched Terrell into the living room. "Have a seat, Terrell. Sit there and don't move," Wilfred barked as he pointed the dagger toward the couch. "And just in case either of you thinks this knife won't do the trick, I've also got a little heat packed away, just for the occasion."

He smirked and opened his leather bomber jacket, revealing a large black semiautomatic pistol neatly tucked away in his waistband.

"Now, first I'd like to ask Terrell a question. Terrell, in your relatively short and miserable life, have you ever seen anyone murdered right before your very eyes?"

"No," Terrell replied nervously.

"Well, just to make sure you don't miss anything, I'm going to see to it that you don't move. Put your hands and feet together."

Wilfred leaned over, retrieved a roll of tape from his jacket pocket, and duct-taped Terrell's hands and feet tightly together.

"Ahh, it hurts!" Terrell cried out.

"You're hurting? What happened, dude? I thought you were supposed to protect her, be her knight in shining armor and all that bullshit," Wilfred said.

I'd wished badly that I could high-jump from my wheelchair and throw him out the fucking window, head first.

Wilfred then leaned in close to Terrell's face as he lay backwards on the couch. "Do you know what I think? Huh, Terrell? I think you're a wuss. Yeah, a fucking wannabe hero."

My eyes welled with tears. Something told me this might be it. I might die here tonight at the hands of this mindless piece of shit. And Terrell might die as well if I didn't think of something quick.

"And now, back to our regularly scheduled whore-gramming."

Wilfred stood up and fixed his gaze on me. "First off, I heard everything! How you talked about me and my mother, who would still be here today, if you weren't such a dumb, selfish bitch!"

"How... did you hear?" I asked, quivering.

"Because I live right fucking next door, that's how! I've followed you, tried to be close to you in case there was some incredibly minute chance that we could get back together. And you cheated on me, too? After all I had invested in you—in us!"

"Well, we could... we could... um... work it out if you'll give me a second chance," I whimpered.

He laughed. "A second chance? Are you kidding me? Whores don't get second chances. You had your chance and you blew it! I killed those other skanks to take away my rage, my hatred for women after what you did to me! You know, Alexis, it's skanks like you who give doctors a bad name."

He set the knife down on the table. "Oh, and I took care of that prick of a coworker of yours, just in case you're wondering."

"You're sick!" I said, shaking my head.

"So, for all of your lies, your crimes against humanity and me specifically, it's payback time!"

Wilfred smiled wickedly and began walking toward me.

"No, please, God, no!"

He grabbed the handles of my wheelchair and forcefully rolled me into the kitchen. I gripped the sides of the doorframe, frantically trying to stop him from pushing me any farther.

Wilfred then yanked my arms away and violently shoved the wheelchair forward, catapulting me to the floor.

"Please, don't do this!" I begged him.

"You remember what I told you in front of your house that day, when I said, 'it's not over'?" he said.

Before I could say anything, Wilfred walked closer and viciously kicked me in the stomach as I lay on the floor.

"Today, you will feel what it's like to suffer slowly and painfully, sweetheart. We're going to start by repurposing that pretty little face of yours." He started opening cabinet doors above the stove and around the kitchen. "Where are the pots?" he snarled.

"I'm not telling you!" I cried, and wondered where the hell the FBI was.

Wilfred walked over to me, towering over my body as I lay holding my aching stomach. Then he knelt down, grabbed my head and started bashing it against the floor.

I started losing consciousness. The room was spinning. I moaned as the back of my head smashed against the ceramic tile.

"Now, let's get some water going on that stove," I could vaguely hear him say.

Slowly, I opened my eyes and could see him grabbing a stainless steel stockpot from one of my cabinets. He ignited one of the stove's front burners. Then he went to the faucet and began filling the pot with water.

Out of the corner of my eye, I saw some movement in the living room. I turned for a brief look.

Apparently, Terrell had freed himself by slicing the duct tape with the knife that Wilfred had dumbly left behind. Terrell looked at me and put his finger to his mouth to shush me from starting to speak.

He bent over to remove the magazines from and then grab the wrought iron rack next to the TV stand.

Terrell slowly crept into the kitchen with the metal rack in his hand, and my heart raced wildly as I watched him raise it high in the air.

Just as Wilfred turned away from the sink to put the pot on the stove, Terrell lunged and crashed the rack into Wilfred's head.

Wilfred went sailing backwards, slamming into the granite countertop. He yelled in pain as the enormous pot fell free from his hands. Water gushed over the kitchen floor.

I turned over onto my hands and knees to put more distance between myself and Wilfred. "Hit him again!" I screamed, wanting Terrell to finish the job.

Terrell rushed forward and whacked the iron rack into Wilfred's skull a second time as he collapsed onto the floor. I could see blood streaming down his face now.

He lay there grunting, his head and back up against the cabinetry. "It's still not over, bitch," he murmured slowly as he turned to glare at me.

Suddenly, I recalled the gun he had boastfully displayed in his waistband, and crawled back toward him to grab it. But before I could get close enough, Wilfred went for it himself, his hand wrapping around the butt of the gun. Terrell lunged forward and smashed the rack into him a third time.

That blow really stunned him, and his head smacked backwards into the cabinet door beneath the sink. While he lay there dazed, I managed to grab the gun from his waist. I wormed away on my hands and knees, still holding it.

"Step away!" I yelled to Terrell. He cautiously stepped back from the kitchen, holding the magazine rack in his hands.

I lay on my stomach facing Wilfred, propping myself up on my elbows, holding his gun in my hands. "Terrell, I've got another gun on the top shelf of the closet in my bedroom. Go and get it! Hurry!"

Terrell darted into the bedroom to retrieve my semiautomatic. I kept my focus on Wilfred, who had started to come to from the blows he'd so rightfully been given.

I nervously looked at Terrell as he returned with the gun. "Take the safety off, grab the phone and call 911 on speaker," I told him.

Wilfred started to lift himself up from the floor, grabbing for the top of the counter. His face was completely covered with blood now.

As I kept my focus on Wilfred, the 911 dispatcher answered the call.

"Nine-one-one. What's your emergency?"

"Please send all available units to 509 East Walton Street, Unit 506. I've just killed an intruder!" I cried.

The dispatcher kept talking, but her voice had momentarily gone mute as far as I was concerned. Wilfred was standing now, looking around the kitchen for some sort of weapon, I presumed.

"Don't do it, Wilfred. It's over now," I told him.

"Uh-uh, not by a long shot," he replied, wearing that stupid smirk of his.

My hands were trembling. I still felt the pain in my legs and stomach from my injuries.

He looked to his left and opened the drawer that I kept my knives in. He reached in and grabbed the largest one, a twelve-inch butcher blade, and twirled it in his right hand.

Then he glared at me, his eyes fierce with hate. "You know, Alexis, you're such a skank. You didn't have the fucking guts to tell me you were seeing someone else!" His head twitched. "And you know what? I believe that neither you nor this little punk has the guts to pull the trigger."

"I don't want to do this, Wilfred. But I will," I warned.

"Fuck you!" he snarled. His face distorted into a pucker of disgust.

Suddenly he rushed forward like a bloodthirsty, stark raving mad wild bull.

Terrell and I squeezed the triggers on the guns we held, releasing a hellish barrage of bullets into Wilfred's face, neck, stomach and groin.

He staggered, clutching his chest and stomach, his blood spurting to the floor. His eyes rolled backwards into his head just before he came crashing down face forward and slammed into the ceramic tiled kitchen floor with a bone-chilling thud.

Terrell and I lowered our weapons. I lay on the floor, my heart still beating rapidly.

"Let me help you up, Ms. Alex." Terrell set the gun down on the kitchen table, stood over me, and cupped his hands under my armpits to pull me up and settle me into my wheelchair.

"I'm sorry you had to go through this, Terrell," I managed, short of breath.

"It's okay," he said nervously, gently patting my shoulder.

Suddenly, an army of cops flooded into the condo, followed closely by FBI Special Agent Preston Ponder and his counterparts. They were heavily armed and dressed in dark tactical gear.

"Are you okay?" Ponder asked. "For some reason the video transmission wasn't working properly."

"I am now," I replied, wiping my eyes and running my fingers through my hair. "I wondered what the hell happened to you guys."

"Sorry we couldn't get here sooner. I feel bad about it!"

Terrell slowly wheeled me into the hallway while the police and EMTs did their thing inside, collecting evidence and removing Wilfred's lifeless body.

Other residents in the building nervously ventured into the hallway after hearing the gunshots, including several elderly neighbors who'd almost gone into cardiac arrest, they told me. I apologized and assured them they were no longer in any danger.

And neither was I.

I could finally take a deep breath, and felt at least some degree of comfort, knowing that this loathsome part of my life was finally over.

The next phase had just begun.

CHAPTER **24**

"I love you all!" I joyously called out to my family, friends and coworkers sitting at decorated tables around the beautiful wood-paneled room we'd reserved at Maggiano's downtown.

Camera flashes lit up the dining area like it was a red carpet event, and Rick Braun's "Tijuana Dance" was playing in the background as I made the rounds, greeting my guests.

It was a chilly but festive night on Clark Street, several days before Thanksgiving. My mother, my best friend Carol and her brother Jason had driven up from Madison to attend.

Also invited were Terrell and his parents and Lou Haney, the smooth-talking detective from Madison. Their presence here tonight meant the world to me.

After all I'd been through, I had a good reason to celebrate.

Damn the cliché, but today *was* the first day of the rest of my life. And I couldn't wait to share it with the people dearest to my heart.

"Mom, come over. I have someone I'd like you to meet," I said, beaming as I waved.

My mother stood up from her seat and walked to the end of the table to meet the special guest I had invited.

"This is FBI Agent Preston Ponder."

"It's a pleasure to meet you, Dr. Fields."

"Likewise. Alexis has told me how much you and the FBI have helped her, and I want to personally thank you for it."

"The pleasure's all mine. It's what we do," he said, smiling. "I'm glad we could finally close this ugly chapter in her life."

"Absolutely," my mother said, then suddenly turned toward the front of the restaurant and back to me, beaming.

I knew that look. I'd seen it a million times. It meant Mommy Dearest was up to something.

"Excuse us, Agent Ponder. Okay, now, Alexis, I want you to follow me. I've got a surprise for you," she said. "But first, close your eyes. I'll guide you."

She grabbed my hand, and we zigzagged through the crowd, the wait staff, and the giddy couples out on what seemed like first dates. We quickly headed toward the entrance of the restaurant.

After an abrupt halt, we both stood silently, and my mind began to wander. "Now, open your eyes," Mom said.

My eyes flew open, and I broke into a huge grin. "Oh, my God! John, what a surprise!"

My mother had secretly invited John Hill, my running buddy from Lake Park. We'd been through hell and high water together, and it was wonderful to see him again.

He'd told me that he couldn't make the trip, citing his new gig with some health start-up in Milwaukee. Apparently, that was all part of the "plan." I wrapped him up in a big hug. We talked for several minutes before I escorted him back to our own private little shindig.

After John had settled into a seat at my table, I walked away for a brief moment to give the DJ we'd hired a special request. Carol and Jason had suggested it was time for some type of line dance, something that could definitely liven up the room.

I walked toward my mother and Agent Ponder and grabbed their hands to pull them out onto the floor space that had been cleared for dancing.

The DJ cued the mega-hit "Blurred Lines" and had everyone bouncing in their seats.

"C'mon, you squares, get up here and show some love for our girl! Let's make this a night to remember!" Jason shouted as he waved his hands, holding a sweaty bottle of Birra Moretti. Most of the guests obliged and headed for the makeshift dance floor.

All in all, it was a beautiful occasion. And we ate, drank, and partied up the rest of the night.

ABOUT THE AUTHOR

ALEX DEAN is the author of *Restraining Order, The Bogeyman Next Door* and *Stalked.* He is an entrepreneur, former musician, and self-proclaimed health enthusiast who enjoys being creative. He writes thrillers as well as other sub-genres of fiction and lives in Illinois with his family. For previews of his upcoming books and more information about Alex Dean, please visit alexdeanauthor.com.

If you want to get an automatic email when Alex's next book is released, you can sign up at alexdeanauthor.com. Your email address will never be shared and you can unsubscribe at any time.

Word-of-mouth is crucial for any author to succeed. If you enjoyed this book, please consider leaving a review at Amazon.com, even if it's only a line or two; it would make all the difference and would be greatly appreciated.

ACKNOWLEDGMENTS

I would like to thank God for his many blessings, a heartfelt thanks to my wife and my parents for their valuable feedback, my children and family for their love and support. A big thanks to my in-laws for supporting my endeavors, and many thanks to my readers for your continued support.

9 7 8 0 9 9 0 5 2 8 1 2 8